Beautiful Monsters

Way Beyond the Sky, Where Dragons Rule, Volume 1

Jeri Andrew

Published by Jeri Andrew, 2023.

BEAUTIFUL MONSTERS

First edition. September 11, 2023.

Copyright © 2023 Jeri Andrew.

ISBN: 979-8223487692

Written by Jeri Andrew.

Table of Contents

Dedicated to my Drew. There would be no series without you.

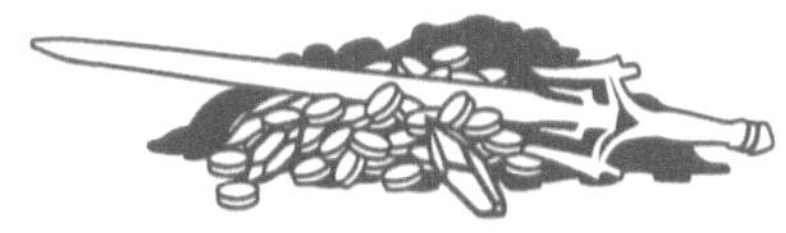

IN THE BEGINNING

In a galaxy some 9 billion light years away from the Milky Way, a galaxy that is home to planets such as Taurus 9, Polaris 8, Earth 8, and trillions of trillions more, many of which are inhabited—too many to count, a small research moon, Ion 6, located in the Pluron Galaxy, and orbiting the planet, Zenix 6, became home to one of the most powerful creatures in existence.

Her parents were the product of human genetic experimentation.

Her parents were two creatures, never meant to meet, much less breed. But meet they did. In doing so, a creature was produced unlike any creature in all of creation, a unique and all-powerful being.

These are the chronicles of the life and times of the infamous, all-powerful,

Queen AlaHanDrea.

Chapter 1

It was an odd day. Of course, lately, all the days had seemed strange.

Something seemed a bit off; nobody could pinpoint it, but everyone felt it.

The inhabitants of Ion 6 were somewhat accustomed to things being odd, given it was a research moon and barely inhabitable.

But this type of o was almost a sense of impending doom. It was hard to describe and had everyone feeling a bit on edge.

Folica was a curious young woman created in the lab by research scientists.

Considered one of the researchers' success stories, the young lady was the result of gene-splicing experiments—species blending, to be exact.

Being of no specific species, the young lady was the only one of her kind.

Folica was a creature of considerable power; she didn't know or understand how to use it.

When the young woman used her magic, she thought nothing of it, believing it to be the usual way of things, with no one around to tell her differently.

Most of Folica's contact with life forms capable of speech was limited to the scientists or caretakers, and neither were very talkative.

Most of the creatures in her area of the research facility were primates, which weren't the most social creatures with non-primates.

Folica was very lonely and starved for affection as well as attention.

Telling the curious young lady something was forbidden was like telling her to see why that thing was forbidden.

The unusual young lady liked teasingly saying that the scientists accidentally put the curiosity bone in twice when they made her.

Folica's entire life had been in a controlled environment at the lab. There just wasn't much available in the way of company.

Boredom, curiosity, and loneliness led her to pick locks and wander a forbidden area of the research laboratory's grounds.

She didn't understand why the area was forbidden. Determined to discover why it was forbidden, she strolled over for a quick look.

A moment later, she heard someone coming. The startled young lady scrambled to hide herself.

Folica wasn't sure what the punishment would be for getting caught in the forbidden zone, and truthfully, she was in no mood to find out!

Having heard curious noises coming from nearby, a funny-looking young man, even by Ion 6 standards, walked over to the area where the terrified Folica thought she had herself hidden.

"Well, hi there!

You're not doing an excellent job if you're trying to hide yourself. Nope, not at all!

I can see you fine. I'm not here to hurt you; you can come out.

I'm Jeffry. Who might you be?" The strange young man asked the frightened young lady.

"Uh, well, uh... you can see me? Uh, well, hello, I guess I'm, Uh... My name is Folica.

What are you?" She replied

"Well, hello, Folica. That sure is a pretty name.

A pretty name for a lovely creature!

I'm a boy, and you are a girl, from the looks of things. Great combo there, now!" Jeffry told her, trying to be all flirty.

The effort was lost on Folica; she did not know about interpersonal relationships. None whatsoever.

"OK, but you didn't answer my question. What are you?" She insisted.

"Oh, o.k. Well, I'm lots of stuff. I even have a bit of meat-eating plant in my makeup. There are no others like me." He boasted.

"Ya, there is only one of me, too." She replied.

"You sure are pretty!

You're a girl, and I am a boy. Do you want to fool around?" He could tell from the blank look on her face that she didn't know what he was talking about.

"Fool around? What do you mean? In what way? I don't want to do anything to get in trouble. I don't much like being in trouble," she commented.

Jeffry thought for a moment, then said, "Have you not ever had a boyfriend?"

"A boyfriend? What do you mean? I have no friends, not really. Just the attendees, and they aren't very social," she replied.

"A boyfriend is a special kind of a male friend… Closer than just a friend."

"You see, Folica, there's stuff we can do that Involves touching each other, that feels good… things only boys and girls can do together… when they are boyfriend and girlfriend. I want to do those things with you." He gently kissed her. Sparks flew when their lips touched!

"Wow! That was cool! I like that; please do that again," Folica said to him.

Jeffry put his hands on her shoulders, turned her to face him ultimately, then kissed her more passionately. More Sparks flew!

She kissed him back!

He looked deeply into her eyes and said, "Folica, there's much more we can do. May I please touch you under your clothes? Touch your bare skin?"

"Uh, ya, sure, I guess that would be okay,," Folica replied.

Jeffry slipped her blouse off. When she didn't object, he cupped her breasts in his hands.

"That feels nice, Jeffry! I believe I like that."

"I like it too!

You see, there is so much more that we can do with each other. Has anyone ever told you about a boy putting his stick inside of a girl?"

"No! How weird is that?" she exclaimed, feeling quite confused.

"No, I mean his penis stick," he pulled it out and showed it to her. She giggled when she saw it all stiff and swollen up.

Laughter was not exactly the response the young man had hoped for, "It's not very nice to laugh at me when I show you my penis, Folica."

"I'm sorry, Jeffry! I didn't mean to make you feel bad!

So... so, you want to put that where and do what with it, why?" She asked, feeling very confused.

He explained it to her in detail, then took her clothes off for her, sliding out of his clothes, as well.

"Now, I have to warn you, it stings at first! But it's so worth the pain! May I please show

you?"

"Stings? Uh, uh, uh, well, I guess it would be ok... I don't much care for pain, Jeffry," she admitted shyly.

"Okay, fair enough. Well, it was nice meeting you. Maybe I will see you around sometime," he said while putting his clothes back on and turning around to leave.

"Where are you going? Wait, Jeffry, don't go. I like you fine; I don't like stings!" She explained.

"It only stings at first, and only the first few times, then it's all fun from there on out! Once you're open, there is no more pain," he argued. "Folica, I wouldn't hurt you for the world.

I don't know why girls have to suffer pain in the beginning. It doesn't seem quite right to me, but that's just the way it is for all creatures.

It doesn't seem quite fair when you think about it. Something that feels so good should not have to hurt at first.

But you'll want to do this for the rest of your life.

It only hurts at first until you get open. After that, there is no more pain for the rest of your life; it only feels good. All females must eventually go through this or live life without the best pleasure there is," Jeffry said, trying to convince her to let him do it.

"Well, uh, well, uh, ok, I guess it will be ok. I don't like pain, Jeffry! Please be gentle," she replied, much to Jeffry's delight.

The excited young man had the biggest smile on his face! He hadn't expected such an easy conquest. The girl was clueless! He could barely contain his excitement.

It took him a moment to locate the right place for them and make it as comfortable as possible.

He kissed her again, touching her unique places, causing the heat of passion to build...

Jeffry helped her lay down in the nest he had created and began creating a hunger deep inside them both!

The experienced young man introduced the innocent young lady to erotic pleasures!

She wanted more of what he was already doing, so he spent a little more time, allowing her to experience erotic ecstasy twice more.

He was about to show her the part that hurt when the couple heard someone coming!

The terrified young adults reluctantly scrambled to get back into their clothes and ran off in different directions.

As the day progressed, Folica couldn't think about anything other than the strange boy she'd met and the weird but strangely lovely things he was showing her how to do.

She found a private place to be, then began exploring herself... amazed at the feelings... never having realized that kind of physical pleasure was even possible.

Jeffry was quickly becoming an obsession for the curious young woman. She wanted to experience the rest if it felt better than what Jeffry had already done!

Waiting for those scientists to leave for the day seemed to drag on.

Once they finally left, the excited young lady put on a simple sundress, nothing else, picked the lock on the door to the garden area again, and hurried back to where she had met Jeffry earlier.

She waited and waited, but no, Jeffry.

Tears began running down her face. She had counted the minutes to be with him again, hoping he had felt the same way. Disappointed that he didn't, she had herself a good cry, then fell right to sleep.

Jeffry finally showed up to see if she may have returned and found her lying down, sleeping.

She looked so pretty and peaceful.

He decided to do as much as he could without waking her.

Much to his delight, she wasn't wearing anything else when he carefully raised Folica's dress!

She woke up to strange but beautiful sensations. Jeffry was naked, doing stuff with her that felt good!

A fire lit deep inside of her!

Before long, he showed her the part that hurt!

She squealed a bit but didn't make him stop.

As painful as it was, she was enjoying the physical contact enough that the pain was well worth it!

The two of them began meeting secretly every day to play around.

Once the pain quit, the young woman couldn't get enough! She counted the minutes until the scientist would leave for the day.

Both loved the attention and physical affection they received from one another.

Jeffry wasn't starved for attention or affection like Folica was; he just had a huge sexual appetite and craved attention.

Folica loved doing it so much that she began talking Jeffry into meeting her when the scientists were there. They would meet, do it very quickly somewhere they weren't supposed to be, then run off, laughing, in opposite directions...

Jeffry scored big-time points with Folica when he discovered a few places where they could see the scientists without being noticed.

One such place was a rarely used balcony garden area. Folica could be seen up there, leaning on the pony wall. What they couldn't see was Jeffry.

The young man with the raging hormones would get behind her and do it. At the same time, they watched the unsuspecting people below, going about their business without having a clue the couple was watching, having sex with one another.

Most days, the two lovers met early in the morning, just after the scientists returned from lunch, and again in the late evenings. Sometimes, they stayed together all night until the morning, trying not to let the scientists or caretakers catch them.

Being with Jeffry became the focal point of her life early on! Being with him was all she thought about: morning, noon, and night.

Jeffry said he would meet her a few times but never showed up. The next time he saw her, he would offer her some flimsy excuse; if she didn't like it, he felt she was free to quit seeing him... Folica must have sensed that, saying nothing else about it.

When Jeffry failed to show up, she began looking around at other creatures, looking for males who might be able to communicate with her.

She wanted to do it some more, and if Jeffry wasn't around, she wanted to find someone else to do those things with her.

One morning, Folica and Jeffry were involved in heavy foreplay when they had to run to prevent getting caught. Folica hated getting interrupted. She was ready and could barely contain herself.

Her attendant showed up to clean her area and check on her. Folica batted her eyes at the young man, then said, "I don't even know your name."

The young man smiled and said, "I'm Dave. My name is Dave. There's something different about you. You seem, I dunno, different."

Folica asked the young man, "Can you keep a secret? I learned about sex! I know how to have sex! Do you know how to have sex?"

He almost choked on his tea! He wasn't expecting that response! "Someone has taught you about sex? Well, how do you like it?" He asked.

"Oh, I love it! I like it, fine! But I don't have anybody to do it with. Do you know how to have sex and make me enjoy it? I was told not to trust most males because they won't want to satisfy me, only themselves, and I want to be satisfied! I like it!"

"Well, I'm open to having you show me what you like if I fail to hit the right spots... I would be glad to help you out as long as I get to get some, too," he explained. "But we can't get caught! It would be my behind if we were to get caught! No one else can ever know! No one! I mean, no one!"

"Well, you don't have to worry about me telling anyone; there's no one to tell! Anyway, the secret is safe with me!

Meet me up on the balcony in 3 minutes," she said, then hurried off. Dave tidied Folica's space, then went up to the balcony to join her.

The young man surprised her, pulling her into his arms and kissing her with a hungry passion. He showed her things Jeffry never even heard of!

She had to stop herself from making too much noise! The guy was driving her to new heights!

Once Dave had finally finished, he focused on her pleasure several more times before letting her go.

Once they were through, he whispered in her ear, "I'll see you tomorrow at the same time. Only go up one more flight of stairs and meet me up there! You'll like it much better!" The nervous young man slipped away as quietly as he could to avoid getting caught.

Folica was in Heaven!

Of course, she wouldn't tell anyone; there was no one else to know except Jeffry, and she wasn't about to say to him about it!

Jeffry considered breaking up with the demanding girl more than a few times.

Being with Folica made it awfully difficult for him to see all of the other females he enjoyed doing it with.

Folica was consuming most of his time and all of his sexual energy, leaving no power or stamina for him to play with his other females.

Jeffry felt like he had created a monster when he showed Folica how to have sex; the girl wanted him morning, noon, and night! It seemed that was all she ever wanted to do!

It was getting to where if he weren't where she said to meet, she'd start trying to look for him. A few times, she almost caught him in the act!

After missing a meeting with her, he noticed she quit attending their midday tryst. He was relieved, so he didn't question it too much. He brought it up once, and she said the attendant was there, and she couldn't get away, which was the truth, minus a detail or two.

Truthfully, if Dave had agreed to spend more time in her enclosure, she would have quit seeing Jeffry altogether! But she enjoyed having the two males... the sex thing was getting her the attention she so badly craved.

Shortly after starting up with Dave, she began looking at her afternoon attendant. Folica finally screwed up her nerve and said,

"Hello, ya know, you come in here every day, and I don't even know your name!"

"Oh, I'm sorry, my name is Frank."

"Hello, Frank, do you like to do sex?"

"Do what? I mean, well, ya, who doesn't like to have sex?" Frank replied.

"I want to have sex, but there's no one here for me, and I need to have sex. Do you know how to have sex and make it feel perfect for the girl?" she asked the startled attendant.

"I do, but I'll get fired if anyone finds out!"

"I'm not going to tell! Look, I'm going up to the balcony, the top balcony garden; meet me up there, and you can show me what you know; if you want to, please say yes; I need you, Frank," she said, then pulled her dress up then right back down... blushing... the young lady hurried up to the top balcony, very quickly made a comfy bed, not realizing she was using magic to do it... then she laid down and waited.

The anticipation was getting to her, so she began rubbing on herself while she waited. She had her eyes closed, really getting into it, when Frank quietly showed up and took over for her, bringing her to a whole new level of satisfaction than ever before!

The excitement of the whole thing enhanced the experience for the young lady!

Frank was different, rougher, less kissing, more getting down to business!

He taught her new things, like showing her how to use her mouth...

Folica was back in her enclosure waiting for her supper, thinking about her 2-to 2:45 visit with Frank and her 10 a.m. visit with Dave.

When she saw the young man bringing her supper, she hurried to make herself presentable.

Billy was taken off guard when Folica blurted out that she wanted to have sex. Billy took her to a private corner of her enclosure, where he knew the cameras wouldn't see them. The excited young man satisfied her several times before having her get on her knees and show off her new skill.

They remained behind that door for only about 7 minutes before they were ready to be seen again.

Billy straightened himself up, patted her on the fanny, and swore her to secrecy before taking off.

The following day, she met with Jeffry as usual, and then she and Dave had a quick mid-morning affair that only lasted about ten minutes.

The hormonal young woman hurried back to her enclosure for Frank to stop by at 2. She loved meeting with Frank!

Billy stopped by about 5.

After supper, she hurried to go meet back up with Jeffry.

As far as she was concerned, every male that got near her was fair game. The young woman had no idea she wasn't supposed to do it with every male that wanted to.

She just loved the attention sex was providing for her!

Loneliness was no longer a part of her life.

Word around the lab's water cooler was, "If you want a quickie, stop by to see Folica." The girl had no clue; all she knew was that she suddenly became quite popular among the male workers.

Folica made up an excuse to Jeffry for missing a weekend with him. He believed her because he wanted to believe her!

It was the weekend.

The scientists didn't show up much on weekends.

Several handlers and attendants went to Folica, explaining that it was like a private club made up of her special friends. It was like having a whole bunch of boyfriends all at once—boyfriends who were all friends. But it was a secret club that no one must ever know about!

Then, they talked Folica into being with a couple of guys at one time while another watched for someone coming, which was no danger.

The young lady didn't know not to; all she knew was that she suddenly had a whole bunch of guys who cared about her and loved being with her for pleasure.

She was suddenly far from being all alone. Truthfully, she would have probably agreed to just about anything her guys suggested to be with them all.

The guys played music, danced with her, and played games with her... they showed her a game called Toss the Beanbag. Every time she missed the target, she had to remove an article of clothing and drink a shot of alcohol.

She was only wearing a skirt, top, and a pair of panties; it would have been a short game, so, once she was naked, when she missed the target, she performed a sexual act of some sort! The guys made the party last...

A little way in, they asked her if another friend could join them. Before the next morning came, six guys were in the room, all making her the center of attention.

She was in Heaven!

It was the most attention she'd ever had in her life!

Having all those guys together was like her own private club; she was the star!

Sometimes, the guys would bring in a new guy or two, making them bring Folica presents if they want to be with her. The new guys were made to pleasure her before being allowed to receive pleasure from her while everyone else watched.

Folica loved her attendants! They promised it would become their weekend thing, making her happier than ever!

She told Jeffry that because her attendants were watching her now, she could no longer meet him on the weekends. He was so relieved! There were not any scientists there on the weekends, so he was able to make his rounds!

Then she told Jeffry she could no longer spend the nights because an attendant was coming in at three and again at 6 a.m., and she would get caught. Again, she didn't lie!

Cam, her new early morning attendant, saw her sleeping in bed.

The temptation was much too significant!

He just climbed in, pinned her down, pulled her gown up, and began doing as he pleased! Never realizing she was agreeable and loving it!

He had planned to smother her dead afterward!

Dead girls tell no tales.

But her responses to him were not negative at all! She was begging him for more!

He got even rougher with her; she LOVED it!

The man gave her all he had to offer, trying to make her fight back... but all she did was want more! By the time he had finally finished, she had him pleasing her multiple times instead of killing her, never realizing he had planned to take what she had and then end her life!

Cam fell in love with being with Folica!

She took what he had, then made him satisfy her!

Anything Folica wanted from then on out, Folica got!

More than a year after they began meeting, the promiscuous young woman quit showing up to see Jeffry in the mornings. She didn't seem up to meeting in the evenings, either.

Her afternoon trysts even became nonexistent.

Worried that Folica had somehow managed to find another male she could be with, Jeffry finally broke down and went to see her, barely missing her morning attendant. He asked her what had changed to cool her towards him.

Folica explained to him that something was wrong with her.

When she woke up, she was sick to her stomach and didn't feel like doing what they normally did.

She said that her breasts hurt, and her tummy felt like something was moving in there! Maybe a bunch of gas or something.

A look of fear on Jeffry's face was confusing to her.

"Why does my being sick frighten you, Jeffry? I'm not dying. At least, I don't think I am!"

"No, you're not dying... But I think you might be having a baby!"

"What? Why would you say such a thing to me?" She asked, feeling very confused.

"Folica, don't you know how babies are made?"

"Well, uh, no, not really. I've never really given it much thought. Why?"

"Well, the things we've been doing can make babies... I thought you already knew that?"

"No, you did not!

You knew I had no idea!

I knew nothing of any of this until you showed me!

Why would you do that to me?

Why would you make me have a baby?

Why would you put a baby in me?" Folica asked, obviously upset.

Jeffry replied, "You said I could! You said I could! I didn't make you do anything you didn't want to do! I asked you first, and you said it was okay

Then, you're always after me to do it again, do it some more!" Jeffry protested.

"But that's because you didn't tell me it would make a baby!"She protested.

"Honestly, I didn't think it would!

You and I are so different!

Our species are so different!

Only one of them is the same!

Why would I think that you and I could make a baby?

Anyway! How would I know about all these things?

We have only one matching species!

I thought that meant we were safe!"

"Well, it looks like you are wrong, Mr. Smarty Pants!

What do we do now??" she asked, tears rolling down her cheeks...

"What do you mean, what do We do? I'm not having a baby; you are!"

Folica slapped his face as hard as she could before running away, screaming, "I hate you!

I hate you! I never want to see you again!"

The following day, Folica went to the scientists responsible for making her, Dr. Jim Shannon & Dr. Lee Kim, confessing everything about Jeffry to them... leaving out the part about her and the male helpers of the lab...

Sure enough, she was pregnant!

The scientists were thrilled! They weren't sure if she could reproduce or if there was a creature for Folica to try to breed with, and that question had just been answered!

Neither scientist was surprised that Jeffry was the father! That horn dog had fathered babies throughout the lab's creature population!

They had baby Jeffry combinations all over the place!

The good doctors explained to Folica that being pregnant was a great thing and that she had to live with the consequences of her actions.

None of that would have happened if she hadn't been hanging out where she didn't belong.

The scientist explained to her that creatures like Jeffry were why that was a forbidden zone—for her own protection!

The scientists explained to her that she had to have the baby. It already lived inside of her. The only other option would be to kill it, which the scientists did not want to do!

Killing the baby wasn't what she wanted to do.

How could she kill her unborn child?

Having to have the baby was not the answer she wanted to hear, either!

She didn't want to have a baby!

Folica had witnessed creatures giving birth and caring for their young, and she wanted nothing to do with it!

Her guys were great with the news! They acted like they were all the father, and who knew for sure?

They explained that being pregnant was the best time to have sex because she couldn't get pregnant while pregnant.

Her fellas also apologized to her for assuming she knew that sex could make babies.

They thought she already knew.

Happy and relieved that the scientist blamed only Jeffry, all her guys stood by her.

Fortunately for the troubled young woman, the pregnancy didn't last too horribly long. Much to her delight, the guys rallied around her, acting excited and happy about the whole thing! She was suddenly receiving loving attention, other than just for sexual pleasures. The guys stayed with her throughout the days and nights, with the blessing of the scientists, who thought it was their idea for the attendants to help keep a close eye on the expectant female.

The expectant mother's emotions were a mix of positive and negative throughout the pregnancy.

There were times she actually was excited about having a child... yet times that fear gripped her so badly, she didn't think she would be able to take another breath.

The good doctors recruited a midwife/nurse, Angela, for Folica, to help during the pregnancy. Folica loved having Angela around. Her company and attention, along with her guys, made the pregnancy actually enjoyable.

Midways through her pregnancy, Jeffry had tried to talk to Folica.

He wanted to tell her that after giving it a whole lot of thought, he was really excited about them having a baby together. He loved her and missed her and wanted to try to raise the baby, just him and her, like a real family. But she didn't want to hear him, not after the scientist told her what they did about Jeffry fathering so many babies, with so many baby mamas!

Plus, the fact that had she known, she wouldn't have been playing with every male in the lab! It was all Jeffry's fault, as far as she was concerned!

He would try to speak, only to have her yell and scream at him to go away, that she hated him and never wanted to see him again.

His head hung low, as he slowly walked off ... crying ... knowing he had really messed up. (Not realizing he wasn't the only candidate for being the father!)

But he just gave up, without trying anymore... Opting instead to feel sorry for himself, knowing the other females would see his sorrow and would want to comfort him...he always had an angle, that one!

The day finally arrived for the baby to be born.

Folica met that day with both joy and sadness, but mostly with fear.

As luck would have it, Dr. Jim Shannon and Dr. Lee Kim, were away on a long weekend, when labor began.

Delivery was not something Folica wanted any part of! She couldn't believe how much pain was involved!

Fortunately for her, labor went quickly and without incident.

Her midwife, Angela, was a goddess of love & passion...

The good doctors had convinced Angela to stay by Folica's side during their absence.

They were sure the young woman was going to give birth to a very special baby, due to the extreme mix of species involved in creating her.

They didn't really want to leave Folica alone, but their trip couldn't possibly be postponed, so, reluctantly, Angela agreed.

Once Angela had tended to the newborns' needs, she cradled the infant in her arms, preparing to hand the baby to its mother's loving arms, but just stood there, singing softly to the infant.

Folica watched in horror, but said nothing to the goddess. She just laid there, watching, as the nurse gradually vanished into the baby! At the very end, just before the nurse vanished, she looked down, seeing herself being absorbed! She screamed, but only for a moment before vanishing into the baby!

The baby girl seemed to have grown. She was sitting straight up, as well as an 8 month old baby would!

She burped and said "Scuse me" and giggled...

Folica screamed!

"Mommy!" The baby said, reaching for her mother, only her mother wanted nothing to do with the child, sure the baby would kill her!

She tried to run away, but the baby would say, "Mommy," and Folica would appear, standing in front of her!

The tiny girl obviously was a baby of magical abilities... using magic to retrieve her mommy.

No matter how hard Folica tried, she couldn't get away from that monster child!

That precious baby girl seemed to always be giggling, cooing and blowing spit bubbles... Content to be checking out the world around her.

It didn't seem to bother her that her mommy was always trying to run away.

Beautiful by anyone's standards, the infant girl was capable of caring for her own needs, from the moment of her birth.

Affection was what she sought from her mother.

When Monday morning arrived, Dr Jim and Dr. Lee Kim were running a bit late.

Folica never wanted to see them as badly as she wanted to see them right then.

She hoped and prayed that the good doctors would relieve her of that murderous monster child!

She was only grateful that the child didn't look to her to be fed... seeming able to take care of her own needs...

Folica watched while the baby turned small animals to vapor, then inhaled the vapor, burped, giggled, then saying, 'Scuse me,' each time...

It was midmorning before the 2 Doctors of Science finally arrived.

They were thrilled to see that Folica had given birth!

The two researchers were only slightly curious as to where the nurse had gotten off to... they were preoccupied with logging data on the baby.

Dr. Jim was busy logging in his journal, while Dr. Kim was checking the baby out.

Folica watched in horror while the baby very quietly turned Dr Kim to Vapor and inhaled every drop, then burped, giggled and said, "Scuse me."

Dr. Jim turned when he heard her speak, at only 2 days old!

He was very surprised that his colleague was no longer in the room. He assumed the man must have gone to the bathroom...

The beautiful baby girl looked up at Dr Jim, smiling, reaching up for him to pick her up.

When he acted as though he was going to ignore her, she began to fuss, "Well, oh, o.k. Come here, I'll hold you, little one," he said to her, as he picked her up, positioning her on his left hip, then turned and continued to write in his journal, "Very beautiful girl child, seems to display more Humanoid characteristics, although she does have wings. She appears as a human infant with transparent butterfly type wings.

At only a 2 1/2 days old, child sits and speaks... the mother seems ok physically, but mentally, seems to be almost incoherent."

Folica just sat, staring, expressionless... in a state of utter shock and disbelief...

Only a few minutes had passed when Dr. Jim reached for his coffee cup, with his left hand... by the time he realized he was no longer holding the baby on his hip, it was much too late! He looked down and saw that he was being absorbed! He screamed just before he vanished!

The baby girl sat where the good doctor once stood. She burped, giggled and again, said, "Scuse Me!"

Folica sat, staring... expressionless...

"Mommy... wuvz me mommy," the baby girl said, giggling, seeming to become more intelligent as well as capable, with everyone she ate or absorbed...

Folica was in a total state of shock and disbelief! Not just fear, but Pure Terror gripped her soul!

A couple more of Folica's men showed up to check on her, having heard that she had delivered the baby. Each one wondering if they were the father.

Folica screamed at them all to leave! She offered no explanation, she just screamed at them! Fear of being found out made them honor her words.

Folica feared for anyone and anything that were to get near the child, especially herself... But she only sat and stared off into space... barely getting up to tend to her own needs... knowing if she tried to get away, the child would just bring her back!

She couldn't believe that she had made her guys leave her alone! But what choice did she have? The baby would have killed them! No, running them off was the best choice, the only choice.

Folica was gone out of the room for only a couple of minutes, before returning to sit, curled up in her hanging, wicker, teardrop chair... gently swinging in the slight breeze, blowing in through the open window of the labs control room.

She was deep in thought... placing the blame for the creation of that baby monster all on Jeffry, as well as the scientists.

Anger and resentment were consuming her, along with self-pity.

The distraught young woman seemed oblivious to the baby, sitting on the bare lab floor, playing with her fingers and toes.

At first, Folica didn't notice the ground fog rolling in, then, quite suddenly, a blinding light appeared! The baby fell over onto her belly, hiding her face from the light, but her mother barely noticed it at all...

"Don't be afraid, I'm the arc Angel, Mitchin. The other angels and I have been observing.

We don't usually interfere, but Folica, you've left us no choice but to get involved.

It's heartbreaking that you don't realize how blessed you are to be the mother of a special soul, such as this little one!

It's a shame that you don't realize that she would never harm her own mother...

When a creature possessing the kind of power this little one possesses comes to be, it draws the attention of both Good and Evil.

Her early years are vitally important, yet her own mother refuses to even give her a name, therefore, the other angels and I, have taken the liberty of choosing her name.

Queen AlaHanDrea, Gods Special Messenger, Brave and Powerful Warrior, Protector of All..."

The baby girl bounced on her butt, clapping her tiny hands, laughing and blowing spit bubbles, excitedly approving of her name...

"Folica, you could have had an incredible life as her mother!"

The despondent young mother barely heard his words. She wondered how life could be so twisted and cruel... Had this angel only shown up 15, maybe 20 minutes ago!

It was already too late.

The terrified and distraught young woman could feel the poison coursing through her veins.

Death came Quickly.

"Mommy!

No!

Oh Mommy, mommy, mommy... got you mommy!" AlaHanDrea could see the spirit of her mother standing beside her body.

She reached her arms out towards Folica, opening and closing her tiny fists... Folica's spirit responded, moving next to her baby, then vanished into the baby's body.

The baby queen patted her chest, saying Mommy, Mommy... tears rolled down her chubby little cheeks, as she sung to herself, patting her chest.

Mitchin couldn't even look at Folica's remains.

Self-pity was not acceptable.

Queen AlaHanDrea, at only a few days old, had become guardian of her mother's spirit... in a way, the baby was comforted, knowing she'd never be alone... she had her mother with her and wouldn't have to keep retrieving the woman when she would try to escape. The baby girl would have resisted absorbing her own mother, no matter how much she desired to, but her mother made it necessary. AlaHanDrea was not at all sad about absorbing her mother's spirit. Her problem was solved. She had her mother, guilt free.

Mitchin was relieved to see a parade of tiny Elfen Fairies, traveling down the path, in search of the prophesied orphaned newborn queen...

Relief and gratitude filled Mitchin.

He knew the fairies would be loyal to the magical infant.

The tiny creatures froze when they saw Mitchin.

"Fear not, tiny ones. I am the angel, Mitchin, servant of God."

The leader of the fairies, Bronah, stepped forward, "you have come to collect the mother?"

"No. The mother committed an unforgivable sin, she committed suicide, no, I came here to give the baby her name.

She is Queen AlaHanDrea.

A name fitting to one such as her.

The worlds are dangerous places for all creatures, but especially to a creature possessing the infinite power of this child!

She must be given guidance, love and affection.

She must be provided good examples of right and taught that evil is the enemy of All creatures and of all life."

Bronah held his shoulders up and said, "stories of her coming, have existed for as long as our memories have existed.

Stories of her have been passed down through the ages.

For as long as Fairies exist, she will not ever be alone."

Mitchin smiled and said, "I believe your words to be true.

Think for a moment, if you will, a creature as powerful as she, at two and a half years old... now, think again of a creature as powerful as she, at 15 years old, full of raging hormones..."

Bronah thought for a moment and said, "uh, good point.

This is a huge undertaking for creatures as tiny as we...

I know just who to call.

The Princess Athena, daughter of King Neptune, God of the seas.

Princess Athena possesses great power.

I'm sure she will be able to be of assistance."

Mitchin smiled at the thought of Athena.

Her beauty was legend!

No man could resist her, not even an angel!

Bronah called out, "Athena!" The rest of the fairies called out her name in unison. No response.

The baby tilted her head back and called out, "Afweeenah!" Then giggled and blew spit bubbles.

A pool of water appeared, churning and bubbling, signaling the arrival of magical creatures from the sea.

Mermaids began to surface, hopping up onto the side and putting their drylander legs on... Once they were on dry land, Athena came up out of the water in all of her beauty.

She had her drylander legs on as soon as she came out of the portal to the sea.

The presence of the angel had Athena putting a white wispy gown on to cover her nakedness, out of respect to him, as well as to God.

"Well, hello baby girl. Aren't you a precious one! You don't know this yet, but I'm your best friend! I've come to help you, while you grow up into an adult, so we can hang out!

We're going to have so much fun over the centuries to come! Yes, we are! I've been dreaming about you for a very long time, yes, I have. Now, I see that you are real, and you are here, as a newly born baby!

Worry not, little one, your Athena is here!" Athena had such a beautiful smile.

The baby bounced on her butt, laughing and clapping her tiny hands together, then said, " Afweeenah, Afweeenah! My Afweeenah!"

"Yes, baby girl, I'm your ATHENA".

"Afweeenah!" the baby said.

"Well, hello there, Angel...?" Athena said more as a question.

"Hello, I'm Mitchin" he said, stumbling over his words, blushing in the presence of such beauty.

"Well, hello, Mitchin, nice to know you.

Tell me Mitchin, why do you name her

Queen?" Athena asked...

"Yes, well, as you well know, she is made of many species. The scientists retrieved DNA samples from many creatures, all of her donors being of royal blood lines... as you, yourself, are well aware.

Your own DNA was used, along with many others, in creating this child's mother.

She is one of a kind and will be the mother of her nations, therefore, she is born as a Queen," Mitchin explained.

"She's of my own bloodline... she shares my personal DNA, through her mother. Interesting," Athena remarked.

Bronah stepped forward, "the DNA of fairies was also used in the creation of her mother... according to our prophesies, she is the salvation of many creatures. She will unite us all, to defend ourselves against our 1 common enemy.

We are taught that she will be the reason we don't become extinct when our world ends.

Her coming, tells us that the time grows near when our moon will be no more... the time to be moved approaches...the time of change is upon us."

Chapter 2

Mitchin heard them first, an entire pride of lions were coming up the path.

The Angel knew they were coming to pay their respects to Queen AlaHanDrea, but the fairies didn't!

The sound of the cats approaching had the tiny ones fluttering in ever which direction, looking for a suitable place to hide.

Mitchin tried to calm them, "Relax, my tiny friends, they've come to greet the newborn queen.

They mean you no harm. Y'all are brought together by Queen AlaHanDrea, they are now, your allies."

His words seemed to calm them down a bit. But then, who doesn't trust an angel?

King Leon the 3rd, walked right up to the baby and laid down in front of her, giving a soft roar... Pretty much ignoring the Angel in the room...

"Wions, my wions, I wubs my wions," the baby said as she reached for the king...

King Leon reached over and pulled her close to him, with his big, soft paws. The precious baby snuggled up to him, cooing.

She spotted Prince Leon, a cuddly playful looking cub, and smiled the prettiest smile. "Babay weon babay weons... My babay weons"... King Leon smiled and said, "he's my cub, baby girl. You and he will be best friends..."

Once Queen AlaHanDrea settled down a bit, King Leon shifted to human form, picked up the baby and cradled her in his arms. The beautiful baby girl squealed with delight, watching him shift!

It was important to the baby for her creatures to be able to look like her at times...

Queen Leonora also shifted to human state, further exciting the tiny baby.

That sweet little baby loved her creatures looking like her.

The rest of the pride followed suit, shifting, looking like the newborn queens tribe.

The entire pride of newly developed shape shifters, took turns passing the baby around, making a big fuss over her, while the king and queen spoke with Mitchin, Athena and Bronah.

"King Leon, first of all, I love the look! Did the baby girl do that for y'all?"

"She did, yes, she sure did. I kind of like it. I wear it well, do I not?" Leon asked, playfully.

"You do, yes, you certainly do," Athena agreed.

"Um, I don't mean to try to tell you how to handle things, but if I were you, I wouldn't be for allowing everyone to hold her.

She is a very dangerous and powerful creature. Alerted by very vivid dreams, I've been watching since just before her birth.

She has already eaten or absorbed a goddess, two scientists, several attendees, a housekeeper, and a multitude of small animals.

If she gets hungry, she will eat.

She is far too young to know not to kill those she sees as food...

She also has the power to absorb creatures ... if she senses power she wants, or knowledge, she will not hesitate to absorb the creature. Absorbing a goddess and a scientist is why she is as advanced as she is at such a young age," Athena warned.

King Leon wasted no time in cautioning his pride to handle her with extreme caution!

Athena looked at Mitchin and said, " So, Mitchin, are angels allowed to..." She was interrupted by Mitchin, clearing his throat and coughing.

"Princess Athena, you are an incredibly gorgeous woman!

No man could resist one such as you!

Not even an angel is immune to your beauty and charms"... he blushed a deep red and vanished!

Athena giggled to herself for having made an angel blush. She Loved the power she had over males, as well as some females...

The princess of the deep looked around at all of the creatures that had arrived to help care for the baby girl.

It was comforting to see so many.

"Bronah, y'all seem to have things well under control, I'm going to go home and speak to my father about the baby.

If you need me, don't hesitate to call on me. Either my servants will come, or I will... Or both.... "

"Good enough, ya, the cats seem to be keeping her attention for now. She's probably getting hungry, though. What should we do about mealtime," Bronah asked.

Before Athena could answer, a family of bears entered the compound. They had also come to see the newborn Queen.

Athena wasn't surprised that it was the royal family...

AlaHanDrea got extremely excited when she saw the bears, reaching for them to come pick her up.

Princess Celina, the daughter of King Bjorn of the bears, went to her, picked her up to cradle her, offering her a breast to drink from. The mama bear had to squirt a bit of milk into the baby's mouth to make her understand, but once she did, AlaHanDrea latched on and went to town! She finished all of Celina's milk, then, finished all of another mama bears milk, before burping and falling fast asleep.

"Like I said, call me if ya need me," Athena told Bronah.

The fairy king said, "Be sure and tell your dad I said hey."

The leader of the fairies was quite relieved when he saw the mama bear successfully feed the orphaned queen.

It was so sad that Celine and her best friend had lost their cubs so tragically...... it was good for them to have a baby to feed, even if she was a species of her own...

Mother's milk or no mother's milk, still, the fairy king knew the child would be wanting protein soon.

He and a group of fairies decided to go catch a supply of creatures for food.

Bronah didn't worry about the baby, as long as the bears and lions were there to protect and comfort her.

With the fairies off hunting and the baby sleeping, bears and lions alike fell asleep for a good nap.

AlaHanDrea's nap was disturbed by the sound of someone in trouble!

She quietly and clumsily crawled away from the lions and bears to go look for the source of the cries. She was far from mastering transporting herself, at only 2 days old, but the cries for help were fueling her determination.

What she discovered horrified her!

Her precious fairies were caught in a web!

Not just any web, but the web of the giant spiders!

All creatures were terrified of those horrible, murderous, venomous beasts!

They were giant by everyone's measure!

As well as ferocious, showing no mercy to their prey.

The baby queen crawled over to the web and very carefully managed to free the fairies, as the spider made its way towards the intruder that was stealing its lunch!

The tiny fairies flew away as quickly as they possibly could, but soon realized that the baby wasn't with them!

The tiny creatures flew high in the sky to see what they could see... The baby was still by the webs, and she was poised to do battle with the approaching angry spider!

At only 2 days old and as tiny as she was, she was prepared to do battle with those horrid creatures!

Much to his horror, Bronah saw the spiders readying to attack... He screamed for the baby girl to run away.

He felt so helpless!

He was no match for even one of those hell beasts!

The distraught leader of the fairies watched in horror as the 8-legged beast jumped towards the infant girl, then stared in amazement when the oversized arachnid exploded in mid jump!

2 more of the vile creatures were running up on her, when their heads fell from their bodies and they collapsed, dead.

The baby giggled and said, " spidows yuck!"

AlaHanDrea quickly created a force field around herself, then began killing spiders as quickly as she could, as an entire cluster came running towards her!

The infant warrior queen made motions with her hands and the deadly arachnids would fall apart into many pieces...

Her stare was blowing them into unrecognizable pieces!

The commotion woke the bears and lions from their naps.

They heard the tiny fairies screaming in terror for the baby, quickly becoming surrounded by the giant, poisonous arachnids!

Instinctively, they ran towards the danger, even though those spiders equaled certain death for both species!

By the time they got close enough to see the baby queen, over 30 spiders lay dead.

They stood, staring in amazement, as the baby made short work of the giant beasts!

Rustling in the bushes let them know that the battle was not over!

Lions and bears usually did their best to avoid the horrible 8-legged beasts, fearing their venom most of all!

Yet there they were, in line to be attacked, due to their curious and protective natures...

Neither the bears nor the lions knew what to do to protect themselves from the approaching creatures!

As mighty as they both were, they were powerless against the spiders' venom!

AlahanDrea was furious when she saw the spiders threatening her lions and bears!

She quickly threw a force field around her fur family and began exploding spiders!

The 8-legged monsters would jump at them, bouncing off of the force field, so they began attacking the force field itself, causing it to begin to weaken!

King Leon and King Bjorn combined magic to strengthen the shields!

Both kings were formidable creatures, Brave... Strong... Very capable warriors, with above average magical abilities... But these spiders... these particular, giant, venomous spiders, struck fear in the hearts of All creatures... All but one, it seemed...

The eight-legged beasts had met their doom with the Baby, Queen AlaHanDrea!

Fearing the forcefield wouldn't hold, AlaHanDrea leaned forward onto her tiny hands and pushed herself up to a standing position. Her chubby little legs were wobbly at best, and she plopped back down on her butt, giggling, then leaned forward onto her hands and pushed herself up again falling again!

She sat, inhaling long and slowly, blowing a wind so cold it burned blue flames!

The spiders froze on contact!

The baby warrior queen took another deep breath, letting out a scream that shattered the horrid frozen beasts!

The giants that had not been affected by the frozen fire, flew backwards when the power of her scream hit them, slamming them into the rock walls of the hills, killing most of the beasts.

Those that survived limped away as fast as they could go...

But the baby wasn't letting them go!

She was determined and on a mission!

That day was their day to die, and she made sure that they did just that!

Once the tiny warrior queen was satisfied that she had conquered the threat to her beloved fur family and fairies, she began giggling and said, "Spidows go bye bye! Bye bye, Spidows! You dead now! Bye bye!" Exhausted, AlaHanDrea created a force field for self-protection, then surprised everyone when she spun a cocoon around herself, falling asleep almost instantly.

Athena had been using her spy cam to keep watch over the baby.

When she saw that newly born girl poising for battle against the giant arachnids, she swam as quickly as she could, trying to get to the baby... although... she wasn't really sure what she could have done about the situation... mermaids were no match for giant spiders, who, had quite a taste for seafood!

But, by the time she arrived, all that was left of the threat, were bits and pieces that used to be spiders... That, and a baby, asleep in a cocoon.

Ground fog appeared around the same time as Athena's arrival.

Mitchin hurried over to King Bjorn and King Leon, "Wow! I know y'all just saw what I saw, but Wow! Did y'all just see what I saw? Uh oh! 3 spiders got away, and they are headed this way!" Athena stepped forward, "Worry not, I've got this one!

Well, with a little help from my friends!

Fairies! Fairies, on my mark, cocoon!" Athena ran ahead a little, towards the approaching beasts, releasing a glittery looking substance into the air that lingered... Once the spiders ran through it, they froze in mid motion, temporarily paralyzed! "Fairies! Cocoon!" She yelled.

Moving as quickly as they could, the tiny creatures spun the strongest cocoons they could spin... Entombing the beasts.

King Bjorn was impressed, as were the others. He looked at Athena with an expression that showed he was very impressed with the princess from the deep, then asked her, "o.k. they are incapacitated for now, but what happens when the magic wears off?"

Athena had a smug smirk on her face, "oh, I thought I'd make a scientists day and sell them 3 slightly damaged, giant, venomous arachnids! I'm sure they will know what to do with them!"

Her response brought much needed laughter to the group.

Athena was right, she Did make the scientist day! It wasn't often they received giant deadly arachnids! Especially Gift wrapped!

Athena looked at Mitchin and said, "Amazing what we can accomplish when we work together!

Teamwork is the key!

I have but one question for you... Dude, you are an Angel!

You hold the power!

You saw what was going on!

Why didn't You step up and put a stop to it?

She's a newly born baby!

What's the matter with you?

She could have been killed!

Many of us could have been killed!" Her frustration was more than obvious.

"Are you done?

Yes, I'm an angel!

We observe!

We are not supposed to run interference when freedom of choice doesn't work out well for y'all!

How are y'all supposed to learn if we run around fixing the scrapes y'all get yourselves into?

It's not our Job!

Anyway, she had this one!

Newly born or not, she freely chose to fight those creatures!

She could have run away. She had plenty of time to escape after she freed the fairies!

That baby girl stayed and waited for them to attack her!

She Wanted to fight them!

You should have seen how smug she was before she cocooned herself...

She knew exactly what she was doing, and she killed an entire cluster!

By herself!

She didn't require Devine intervention!

She IS Devine intervention!

The only ones that got hurt today, were the spiders!

And hey, all they were doing was trying to eat.

Today, it cost all of them their lives!

Truthfully, I feel kind of sorry for the spiders!

They had no idea the threat they were up against...

They were simply hungry...

Predator and prey...

Now, imagine, if you will, that baby as a full-grown woman...

A full-grown woman with an obvious blood lust, I might add!

That was proven with the spiders!

Now, do you understand God's reasons for wanting her watched?

His reason for a band of angels watching over her?"

"I suppose you're right, Mitchin.

I'm sorry that I yelled at you.

Please, forgive me.

Ya know Mitchin, one such as you, could easily cause even a mermaid to lose her heart and hon, mermaids don't do that sort of thing!

You are one sexy... Uh... Uhmmm... Angel... "

"Athena... oh, Athena!" He said, then vanished...

"Well.... You could!" She said, sure that he could still hear her.

———

Chapter 3

The cocoon began to show signs of opening up...

"Bjorn, look, she's finally waking up," King Leon remarked.

Bjorn went over to the cocoon to inspect and sure enough, it was finally opening...

"You're right this time, Leon, I think she may be finally ready to come out!" Bjorn responded.

A chubby little humanoid baby girl with the rosiest cheeks & lips, the prettiest long, thick, curly, deep red hair & eyes of lime green that had streaks of gold running through, emerged, crawling out from the cocoon.

She smiled the prettiest smile when she saw Bjorn, then reached up to him, the sign for him to pick her up.

She melted his heart in that moment.

Bjorn knew that these were the memories he would always treasure.

All too soon, Queen AlaHanDrea would grow into a woman... A woman that would hold an important role in all of their lives...

And he knew her when...

King Bjorn must not have been moving fast enough for the baby...

She spread her tiny wings for the first time and fluttered up to eye level, kissing him on his cheek, then held her little arms out for him to hold her.

How could anyone resist such a request...

She was only content in his arms for about 2 minutes.

The baby queen squirmed her way up onto Bjorn's shoulders to have a seat.

"Well, alrighty then, are you quite comfortable?" Bjorn asked his tiny passenger, with a chuckle.

She nodded her head, yes and made buzzing sounds, with a great big smile on her face, then giggled, bouncing on her butt up on Bjorn's broad shoulders.

Bjorn just gave a little laugh and took a few steps outside...

AlaHanDrea couldn't believe her eyes!

A multitude of creatures were outside, waiting for her to emerge from her cocoon....

She threw her tiny fist in the air, up over her head and shouted, " Quee Awah Haw Dweeeah!!!

The vast crowd of creatures cheered, roared, whinnied and howled in unison ...

Wolves & bears, centaurs, unicorns and horses, eagles, owls & fairies, leopards, panthers, tigers & lions, crocodiles, Merfolk... all creatures whose DNA she shared, there to welcome the prophesied baby queen into the world, as well as help her to celebrate her first victorious battle!

The only creature who she shared the most DNA with, that was not there, was a human. Unless, of course, the food wagon counted.

Babygirl had a limited vocabulary. She was still very much an infant in most ways.

Standing up and walking were still not something she was ready to do, though she did try!

Bjorn gave her to the ladies so she could be breast fed, assuming she was hungry after having been cocooned for so long...

He was correct.

After being fed by 2 mama bears, she was still hungry.

A food wagon was brought around.

Before anyone could say a word, 2 of the men were turned to vapor and inhaled... Just like that, they were both gone!

The baby girl let out a loud burp, then said, " Scuse me," with the long s sound, then giggled. Everyone there went, "Aaaahhhwww...."

The remaining food offerings clung to the barred walls of the food wagon, in terror...

She let them sit for a little while.... Sat on the floor and played with her feet, finally tipping over onto her back, putting her toes in her mouth...

AlaHanDrea fell back to sleep, chewing on her toes.

The beautiful baby girl woke up feeling cranky and drooling all over herself.

Much to everyone's surprise, the normally cheerful baby began fussing.

Athena sensed the cranky baby and headed for dry land to check on her baby girl...

Even Mitchin came running to the crying baby's side!

No one had ever really heard her fuss before.

She wasn't one to cry.

AlaHanDrea had a way of asking for what she wanted that didn't involve screaming and crying... Until then... She sat on the floor boohooing with drool running down her belly and tears running down her chubby little cheeks.

When mama bear picked her up and offered her a breast, she found out what was bothering the Baby Queen...

Teeth!

Word spread quickly...

Soon, remedies from every species began arriving in hopes of providing the miserable little beauty, some relief from the pain and discomfort...

Athena had a feeling it might be teething issues and brought some herbs from the sea to help with the pain, as well as helping the teeth to come through the skin easier.

Growing is painful no matter who you are!

Athena surfaced to find an army of care takers!

No one had to worry about That baby being neglected!

Royalty from each species made up the main circle of caretakers, along with a mixed species of royal guard detail...

Bonding being the main reason for all of the attention...

AlaHanDrea, the baby of prophesies, was a creature of incredible power. She was extremely dangerous, as well as deadly.

Should she become a problem, there was no one to turn to for help, no one, but God himself! And He wasn't one to interfere.

He's a creator. He creates, then allows that which He creates to live their own lives, as dangerous as that can be...

It was imperative that the creatures endear themselves to her, to the best of their abilities, while she was still a baby.

It was just far too risky to not become close to her.

They needed to give her a reason not to destroy them.

According to prophecies, she was to unite the species, to ensure they not go extinct.

She was a baby of terrifying abilities, yet being close to her was essential for survival.

Being close to the baby queen was like having a rattlesnake around.

You never knew if she was going to strike, you just prayed she wouldn't.

Many referred to her as a baby monster, a very beautiful, baby monster.

Occasionally, she would teasingly call herself a baby monster, just to let them know that she knew what they were thinking.

The human population was not good to her.

They were not friendly, or accepting, in any way.

The human sector referred to her as an abomination, a creature who should not exist.

They deemed her a menace to humanity.

Humans do a lot of stupid things behind fear!

Showing cruelty towards that sweet baby was one of the stupidest things the human inhabitants of ion 6 could have done!

A group of do-gooders attempted to liberate her from her existing home, stating she was an orphaned human in the midst of beasts... so, for her own good, they wanted to put her in a foster home and put her up for adoption to find her suitable parents.

The social workers explained their position with the human appearing creatures, looking as though they were her primary caretakers, then went over to pick up the baby to take her with them.

She ate the social workers before anyone could tell her not to, then burped and said, "Scuse me!" Then giggled.

No more attempts were made to remove her from her home. The humans decided it best to mind their own business where she was concerned!

Morning came and there was no sign of AlaHanDrea! It was if she just vanished!

Teething pains woke the precious baby up. Miserable, she began crawling towards something only she could see. It was a distortion of some sort, in the air, like heat waves, or, an energy field.

The tiny baby crawled right through it, into a beautiful, magical garden, full of thick, blooming foliage of all types and colors.

She sat up, clapping her little hands for a moment, then began crawling again, when a net suddenly wrapped itself around her!

She was trapped, with no way out! She was trapped, her gums hurt and she was scared! The baby queen began screaming and crying.

2 boys, around 11 years old, were out playing their favorite game of Pirates out in their yard, when they saw it!

A strange distortion was in the air, like a wall of heat waves or an energy field.

The pair thought they heard a baby crying. They just looked at one another, shrugged their shoulders, grabbed their play shields and swords, heading through that heat wave wall.

Once they were through the wall of energy, they found themselves in an incredibly beautiful, plush garden. They were in awe of the fragrant, colorful place, right out of a fairy tale.

The 2 boys were slowly walking along, looking around, when they almost stepped on a tiny, little baby girl, all caught up in a net!

"Ah! Look, brother! It's a baby! She's trapped!"

The other brother held up his toy sword and said, "Never fear! Rusty and Ray and here! The mightiest two pirates in all of the lands and seas! We'll save her!" Which, they did. They heard their mother calling, held the baby in their hands and left to go answer mom, only when they passed through that wall, the baby was gone!

They turned around to go back to get her, but the energy field was also gone, as if it were never there!

"No mom, we swear it! There really was a baby girl, she has wings and was all caught in a trap. We saved her! Honest, Mom, we're not making it up! We really did find a baby girl and we really did rescue her," the boys protested.

Mom replied, "ok well, you boys go get cleaned up for supper. You were good boys to save the baby."

The next morning, the boys woke up before the sun, to the sounds of a baby crying. They climbed out of bed, threw on their robes and play time boots, taking off towards the sound of the cries.

Only a short way down the path, there it was again! The energy wall...

The boys passed through to the garden.

And there she was, sitting up boohoo-ing, with drool running down her belly... the baby girl with wings. She looked up at them, bottom lip pouting out, face wet with tears, drool, etc... still sniffing she said, "Wussty & Way? My Wusty & Way?"

The boys smiled at her, "yes, baby girl, we are your Rusty & Ray."

The tiny girl had the saddest look in her eyes, "mouf huts! My mouf huts! Wahhh haa haa!"

"Where's your mommy, little one?" Ray asked her.

"Mommy dead," she cried.

"Oh, poor little baby, I'm so sorry. Where's your daddy?" Rusty asked.

"No know... No daddy. Angew... no daddy," she cried.

Rusty reached down, scooped her up in his hand and started trying to comfort her. "Ray, if I try to take her through to other side, her and the garden both will vanish! She needs us! We stand a better chance, I think, if only one of us goes and asks mom what to do. She feels like she has a fever. I'll stay here with her, I'm not scared."

"Well, ya, o.k, I'll go, but, you had better be here when we get back!" Ray said, sounding nervous.

"No, you can't bring mom! I think she's why we couldn't find it again when we left last time, it's just too risky," Rusty protested.

"Well, o.k, then. Wait right here, I'll be fast," Ray said, then vanished through the wall of energy.

The lights on in the kitchen, meant mom was awake and up. Ray was so relieved he didn't have to wake her up.

As soon as he walked through the door, mom said, "There you are, young man! I was about to start a search! Where's your brother?"

"Mom, we woke up because we heard the baby crying. Honest, mom! We went out to her. Mom, she is so tiny! She couldn't be very old, but, she said our names, sort of. Mom, she says her mouth hurts and she's hot to touch. And mom, she says her parents are dead. Well, no, she said her mommy was dead, no dad, Angel, no daddy," Ray explained to his mother.

She sat thinking for a moment. The way her son had corrected himself, he was telling the real truth, not the pretend truth. She began to suspect her sons had somehow found a magical place.

She looked deeply into his eyes and saw only sincerity. The now worried mom said, "Now son, I want you boys to bring the baby home..." he interrupted her, "that's just it, mom, we can't. We tried to do that already and she vanished."

She thought for a minute, then said, "Go get your wagon and pull it around by the shed door, while I go get some medicine and food for you to take to help her, now go on, and be quick about it, now, scoot!"

"Yes, mom," he was nothing if not obedient, hurrying like his mother said. He sat at the table while his mother quickly packed up food, drinks and supplies from the kitchen, then hurried out to the storage shed, filling his little wagon with supplies.

The backpack she put on him was a bit heavy, but he carried it anyway.

Rusty was surprised and relieved, when his brother returned. Ray did as his mother had instructed, rubbing the babies gums with pain relieving cream, then gave her the fever reducer.... It tasted like candy.

The baby stopped crying.

"Well, come on brother, mom said we should make camp. The baby has a fever and needs looked after.

Mom says she's proud of us for taking care of an orphaned baby," Ray said with pride. "She says we are becoming little men."

The two boys busied themselves putting up their tent, their pavilion cover and building a fire for warmth and comfort.

Both boys were well trained young men in the art of survival. They had been building their own camps since they were 5 years old.

AlaHanDrea sat up watching them, happy that they were planning on spending time with her. She didn't think about anyone missing her, or worrying about her.

Athena was beside herself with worry over AlaHanDrea!

No one could find her!

Creatures from all over were searching for their orphaned and abandoned baby girl, their prophesied baby queen, but there was no sign of her and no sign of anything wrong happening, either!

Panic was setting in, fast!

Hours turned into days, with no sign of what became of their precious baby queen.

THE BABY QUEEN LOOKED at the boys tents, then made motions with her hands to make their tents larger, putting up a bed for herself inside with them.

"Brother, look! She can do magic!" Rusty exclaimed.

"She sure can!" Ray squealed.

"I sweepy," she told the boys, yawning, then threw up. They cleaned her up, then put the diaper on her their mom had given them. She tried to pull it off a few times, then just fell over and fell asleep. The boys picked her up, placing her in her tiny bed, then settled down to get some rest themselves.

The boys woke up to the sound of their father calling. Ray went that time.

Their parents had watched through their crystal ball. They were sure the boys were being truthful. But, for some strange reason, when they walked over to where the entrance should have been, they couldn't find it. They had to go inside the house before Ray could once again find it.

When Ray returned, he found his brother playing with a baby dinosaur and a strange baby gorilla with wings. They quickly became friends with the creatures, as did the baby girl.

After the fist day, the boys constructed a more permanent type of structure, with the help of baby girls magic, that is. It turned out to be a pretty incredible tree house. One the boys loved!

The kids were together day and night, until AlaHanDrea broke her fever. Once she was feeling much better, she knew she had to go back.

The kids vowed to meet in the garden as often as they could.

At first, they saw each other every day, but as time went on, their visits because shorter and less frequent.

Features of all species were assembled together after having turned over every stone, looked in every cave, up every tree, with no sign of AlaHanDrea anywhere! It was if she had just vanished without a trace!

Grief was beginning to take a strong hold on all of those that had come to truly love the baby girl, when an energy field suddenly appeared like a distortion in their air! Energy began shooting out of the thing like lightning bolts from a storm!

The creatures cleared the area, it only enough to feel safe, curiosity kelp them close by. The creatures felt sure the thin g was related to the missing baby, and they weren't wrong!

Thick clouds and fog began to emerge from the distortion, cause the curious creatures to back away. They couldn't tear their eyes away from the distortion for even a second, all but holding their breath in anticipation, eager to know the truth behind the unusual phenomenon.

Sounds like battle sound began being heard! Athena had be held back to be stopped from running into the thing, when suddenly, AlaHanDrea came crawling out from the strange wall of energy that had so completely gained the attention of all who were near.

Cheers rang out, along with applause, as relief flooded across the crowd for the return of their baby

Chapter 4

A few months had passed from the baby queens initial finding of the gardens, when babygirl received a secret visitor about an hour before daybreak.

It was none other than King William, II, of the kingdom of the wolves.

"I'm sorry to wake you, my queen, I come to you with a secret request."

AlaHanDrea sat up, cooing at him.

"Your majesty, I have lived a long and fruitful life. My time approaches rather quickly.

I'm here to request you to absorb me, please.

I am a wolf of great knowledge and power. You will gain so much, with me as a passenger...

So, I implore you to...."

He wasn't able to finish his request ...

AlaHanDrea burped and said, "Scuse me," then giggled and went back to sleep.

She woke up to the ground shaking!

A huge quake struck the moon!

Before she could respond, a huge flat rock fell. The frightened infant caused it to land at an angle, leaning against a rock wall, with AlaHanDrea trapped below.

Tons of rock and dirt fell down on top of the flat rock, entombing the tiny queen.

As soon as she was able to free herself, Athena made her way to the surface.

She was horrified at what she found when she arrived at the babies' home!

A crowd began to gather.

Creatures of all species began digging, moving dirt and rocks, frantically trying to get to the buried baby!

As hard as they all worked, as soon as they would make progress, more dirt and rock would fall, leaving more than there was before!

The creatures just worked harder trying to save the baby!

Then, they heard a tiny voice say, "I wanna hep, can I hep? I can hep! Wet me hep, pweeze."

It was the baby girl!

She was dirty, but alive! And free!

She quickly became surrounded, receiving group hugs and many kisses....

"Oh, precious baby, how did you get free?"

Athena asked her.

"Angew. Angew hep me pop out!" She explained, then vanished. "I up herewu," she hollered, from on top of a high cliff, then vanished and reappeared in front of Athena.

"Nice, very nice!"

Ground fog rolled in. Athena got very excited, until she saw the Angel... "Hello, Athena, I'm Sarafina," the angel introduced herself before the baby butted in... "Sawafweeena! I wubs you, Sawafweeena! I wubs you all much!!! Sawafweeena make me pop out!"

Athena looked at her and said, "Oh! Thank you, thank you, thank you! I don't know what else to say?"

The angel looked at her and smiled, "I know what you want to say, and the answer is, Mitchin is indisposed at the moment.

He's in the process of earning a pass. Seems there's a certain female he deeply desires, and he has requested a much-needed vacation.

You see, God is merciful and a huge fan of love.

He has provisions for when an angel would like to experience life in the flesh...

This will be Mitchin's first time to take vacation.

And I will just bet that you know who this female is," she said with a big smile...

The look on Athena's face was priceless! "Indeed, I do, at that. He's really taking a vacation? Just to be with me?"

"Well, he's taking a vacation to experience life in the flesh. You are what spawned it. I do know that he desires to be with you, to experience you. However, please remember, angels do not often get to take vacations and with this being his first one, there is much he will want to experience while here... please, just don't get your feelings hurt."

"Right. I'll try really hard not to allow my feelings to be hurt, as long as he does the same...

You know, mermaids are not popular for monogamy..." Athena replied, with obvious excitement in her voice.

More Ground fog rolled in...

A voice from behind her got Athena's attention.

She turned around to see Mitchin standing there... "Hello Athena. Check it out, I'm on vacation!

Now, what was it you were saying about a mermaid losing her heart?"

As flesh and blood, Mitchin was a tall, very muscular, quite handsome and appealing man.

Athena walked over to him, gazed into his eyes, then tippy-toed and kissed him on the lips very softly. He took her by the shoulders, then kissed her with a bit of passion. Electricity shot through them both during that kiss!

The baby just giggled and bounced on her little butt with excitement, watching Athena with her angel...

"So, tell me, angel, can you breathe underwater?" Athena asked him.

"I can, but think I would prefer you keep your dry lander legs on for a bit. Can't we find some place to be alone without going under the sea?"

"Oh, I bet we can. Can you still do magic?" Athena asked him.

"Oh yeah, I sure can! Where would I be in this world if I couldn't?" Mitchin asked her, then created a small hut, using his magic.

Athena smiled, took him by the hand and led him inside. She looked around the bare hut and decided it was her turn to use magic.

She opted for a hammock made for 2.

She looked Mitchin in the eyes, it was obvious he was a bit nervous...

"This is the first time you've been flesh?" She asked him.

"Yes, it is. I like it already." He pulled her close, kissed her passionately, then picked her up in his arms, used his magic to create a large, round bed, laid her down, then crawled in next to her.

She acted a bit aggressively, but he rolled her on her back, pinned her hands above her head in a show of dominance, then proceeded to show her that he knew exactly what he was doing!

For an angel, he seemed to possess a great deal of knowledge of the female body, as well as pleasure points, much to Athena's delight.

For the first time in her life, she found herself feeling things for a male that she never thought she was capable of feeling!

Truthfully, it scared her...

But she didn't fight it...

The sound of creatures cleaning up after the quake finally made Athena and Mitchin emerge from their hut.

Both were blushing...

Sarafina grinned, "Well, hello there, you two. Bout time y'all came out..." She teased, then said, "baby girl is napping. Her teeth are making her run a bit of a fever, so I helped her rest."

"Ah, poor baby girl," Athena replied.

Mitchin said, "We should check on families of the dead. That was a powerful quake".

Athena agreed with him, then thanked Sarafina again.

"Think nothing of it. I will stay here by the baby... Y'all go on ahead, there are creatures that need you both..." Sarafina remarked. And she was right.

That quake yielded many casualties of all species.

Cleanup was going to take a while...

Chapter 5

The powerful quakes had erupted all over the moon.

Casualties among the creature population were minimal compared to the human sectors.

Creatures didn't build as many collapsible structures as humans did.

Many of the humans that died, were killed by collapsing structures.

In the past and up until then, quakes were not really a common occurrence on Ion 6... nor were weather phenomenon...

But that had all changed and quite quickly.

No one was certain why...

Thunderstorms had begun to happen with more frequency.

Shortly after the big quake that had trapped AlaHanDrea, a rather large thunderstorm was brewing.

The baby queen became very excited! She could barely hold still waiting for it to arrive. It was to be her first storm.

No one noticed at first, but, as the storm approached, babygirl crawled outside and sat up on top of the highest hill in the area!

The wind began to blow as the storm moved in. She sat with her eyes closed, allowing the wind to blow her face and hair.

The rain began, but the baby stayed on the hill!

Lightning began striking the ground!

AlaHanDrea leaned forward onto her hands and pushed herself up into a stance, raised her little arms towards the sky and began inhaling!

It seemed as though she was sucking in energy from the storm!

King Leon was the first to notice her out there, right about the time lightning was about to strike!

There was no time to react before lightning struck her!

Time seemed to freeze for King Leon! But then, he saw that she was more than alright! She was feeding off of the storm!

That sweet, dangerous, baby girl, was actually feeding off of the energy produced within that thunderstorm!

She seemed to be soaking it up!

Lightning bolt after lightning bolt struck that baby girl, only she seemed to be absorbing all of them!

She seemed to be calling the lightning to herself!

Bjorn, Leon and William IV stood watching as that beautiful baby girl seemed to be absorbing the energy from the entire storm!

They had never seen anything like it, or even heard of anything like it!

The baby queen glowed, as lightning bolt after lightning bolt came crashing down, until the power of the entire storm seemed to disappear into her!

It was, by far, the most incredible thing any of them had ever seen!

Afterwards, she plopped down on her butt, burped and said, "Scuse me," then giggled, as usual, only this time, she peed a stream!

They just stood there, with shocked looks on their faces, in utter disbelief at what they had just witnessed.

William IV, spoke first, "uh, gentlemen, that baby just consumed the energy out of a thunderstorm... I saw her do it!

She ate a thunderstorm!"

"Ya, ya, she did," King Leon replied.

"Are y'all sure we're not dreaming?" Bjorn asked.

"No, we're awake. She ate a thunderstorm!" William answered.

AlaHanDrea got up and started trying to walk back to her favorite three guys.

She kept plopping down on her butt, laughing, then would lean forward onto her hands, push herself back up into standing position and try again, only to take a step, then plop right back down again, laughing.

One of the lightning bolts that had struck the ground, had chased some anzers out of the ground. They resembled big, black or red ants and had very painful stings.

AlaHanDrea saw them coming towards her.

She stared at them, and they began popping like popcorn! She didn't have to kill very many before the rest turned and ran away as quickly as they could!

The baby just laughed at them and kept on trying to walk.

Leon couldn't take it anymore; he walked over and scooped the baby girl up into his arms.

"Good job, baby girl! Very good job! Wow, you ate a storm, didn't you?" He said as he tickled her tummy a little.

She just giggled and nodded her wet head... Then said, "I Quee Awah Haw Dweeeah!" Smiled, then started blowing spit bubbles again.

"Yes, you are! And I Love you, baby girl! I love you sooo much! " Leon told her, then kissed her cheek.

She smiled and blushed a little, then held his face in her tiny hands, kissed his cheek and said, "I wubs my Weon, too! Much much! My Weon! I wubs you," then she laid her head down on his shoulder, hugging him.

"One of these days, you're going to grow up...... Yes ma'am. You sure are."

"I gonna gwow up! I gonna gwow up! " She repeated. Then she wiggled to get down. Once she was on the ground, she wrapped her little arms around herself and began to spin in circles! Seconds later, a full grown, gorgeous woman stood before them!

All three men were in shock and disbelief!

They had not ever seen a woman as beautiful as she!

"Dis me whens ize gwoze up," she said, then shifted back to a baby, sitting on her chubby little butt, blowing spit bubbles.

The three men just stood there, looking at each other, shaking their heads.

"Wow. I mean, wow." Leon said.

"Ya, Wow," William IV said.

Bjorn shook his head and just said, "wow."

All three men excused themselves, in 3 different directions, all 3 shifting back to their natural states as they walked away... A wolf, a lion and a bear....

Chapter 6

Once the men left, Mitchin and Athena walked down to see what AlaHanDrea was doing, playing in the dirt.

The baby was busy making little mountains.

"What are you doing, baby girl?" Mitchin asked her.

She made the first mountain erupt like a volcano, lava flowed down the sides and destroyed everything in its valley.

Then, she showed him the second mountain. It had strange designs carved into it. When it blew up, the lava flowed through the designs cut into the side of the mountain. Then, she showed him a third mountain. Before it blew up, she cut a hole in the side of the mountain. It, too, had designs cut into it. Only, that mountain didn't blow its top off. When the pressure built up, the lava flowed from the vents cut into the mountainside, down through the designs cut into the mountain, preventing the eruption.

Athena remarked, "how about that, baby girl is showing you how to stop volcanic eruptions and decrease quakes... I guess being buried alive motivated her to come up with this.

The question is, how are you going to convince the humans to do this? They are the ones with the technology and the machines.

The secret for saving lives as well as property seems to all be in controlling the eruptions....

Makes perfect sense when you think about it. Smart Kid!"

"How am I going to convince the humans? Why do I have to do it? " Mitchin asked...

The baby girl looked up at him and said, "is you peepow job, angew mishins. Yooze angew is you job...no baby job... Angew job..."

"How about that, she wants you to get a job! Isn't that sweet?" Athena teased

"O.k. well as far as jobs go, I must say, this is a good job for an angel."

"Oh, I've got to hear this presentation! I can't imagine how that sales pitch is going to go..." Athena teased.

"How about I just tell him the truth?"

"Oh, right. You're an angel and an infant girl told you how to fix earthquakes and volcanoes eruptions.

An infant girl that doesn't even know how to walk yet....., Ya, sure, they will go for that first pitch," her sarcasm was very obvious

"Ya, well, the truth is going to have to work... I'm an angel, I don't do the lying thing!" Mitchin replied rather smugly.

Athena said, "This ought to be good!"

"It's all in how you tell the truth, beautiful lady...." He said with a wink and a smile

"BTW, you never did tell me how long your vacation is for..." Athena said with a mischievous grin.

Mitchin's smile widened, "Oh, didn't I? I'm sorry. Ya, it's not a very long one, I suppose it's because it's my first one.... Ya, I've only got 1 lifetime."

"Seriously?" she asked, surprisingly excited by the news.

"Seriously!" He replied with a twinkle in his eye.

Chapter 7

Truth be known, Mitchin was feeling a teeny bit apprehensive over his scheduled meeting with General Williamson.

He'd need to be very careful how he worded things.

The last thing he wanted to do was to come off as some kind of crackpot.

The humans of Ion6 didn't have as good of an understanding of the spiritual world as the creatures did.

Many of them even closed their minds to all things spiritual.

They thought the belief in God and angels to be hokey.

Trying not to stress over it, Mitchin made sure his models were ready, as well as all of the data needed to explain it all, in printed format.

The vacationing angel wanted to be sure he had everything required to convince the humans to do what was best for everyone, not always an easy task...

Taming nature wasn't an easy task, either. He hoped they would appreciate the gift of knowledge he was bringing to them.

Athena swam over to Mitchin's moon home, to offer him support... and she wasn't alone.

She had her little 2 1/2 yr. old brother, Dane, with her. She wasn't really babysitting, Athena truly enjoyed having Dane hang out with her.

The baby queen was excited about Mitchin's meeting. She crawled over to see him.

That baby girl could go far, fast, crawling as well as she did!

AlaHanDrea's intelligence was far beyond her years.

Mitchin was thrilled to see Athena. "Well, hello there, and who is this little man, no, don't tell me... let me guess! It's Prince Dane!"

The shy little merboy was hiding behind Athena... That is, until he spotted the prettiest little baby girl, crawling over to say hello.

AlaHanDrea saw Dane, stopped crawling and sat up, smiling and clapping her little hands, blowing spit bubbles and laughing with excitement.

Dane went over to her, "Hello, I'm Prince Dane, Heir to the throne... My father is King Neptune, God of the Seas. Princess Athena is my big sister. Are you the baby queen everyone's talking about?"

"I babay quee... I quee Awah Hawa Dweeeeaa. You Pwince Daaaa. You Afweeenas' babay bwudda. "

"You sure are pretty for a baby girl and you talk really good, too," Dane told her, then kissed her on her cheek.

She blushed and giggled. So, Dane gave her a peck on the lips.

He got a big ol' smile and a beet red face, for that one.

"AlaHanDrea, can I be your boyfriend?" Dane used his magic to produce the prettiest locket with a picture of both of them in it.

He hung it around her neck and gave her another Peck on her lips. She squealed with excitement, then said, "I you giwalfwin. You my boyfwin," then giggled and kissed her locket.

She used her magic and produced a thick, gold chain to hang around Dane' s neck.

It had 4 flattened nuggets that spelled out DANE. "

Thank you, I Love it! Wow! I will wear it always," Dane told her.

"Auway," she replied, clutching her locket.

"Ah, look at that, Mitchin, puppy love... Aren't they sweet?"

"That's pure love there, now. The purest, most honest kind of love.

Those two kids fell in love at first sight ... As babies... Best friends for life!

I'm an angel, I know these things...

I love witnessing true loves birth!"

"So, what you're saying, is that their love is far greater than puppy love. They actually fell in love at first sight.

The kind of love that never stops ...

They found each other.

Only, mers don't do that sort of thing.

Oh, we love, our love is forever... Just like the love I feel for your angel self, but we don't pair the same as most creatures do...

I mean, we do marry, sure, just not like many creatures do. That's why I'm so perfect for you...

We don't do monogamy.

We don't care who somebody's parents are, we all raise the children. We're with who we want to be with, when we want to be with them."

"That's exactly what I'm saying. He is now Her Dane... She is now his baby queen... Don't even try to get between them...

And you're right, monogamy will never be part of their lives. A creature such as AlaHanDrea, will not ever belong to just one.

Their love isn't about ownership. Their love is forever ....no matter what.

It's the kind of love that comes along very few times in a lifetime...

The kind of love that will grow as they grow and will stand the test of time. They're very lucky." Mitchin explained, then, "Wait, you said you love me... "

Athena acted as though she hadn't heard the last part. "Look at how he's tending to her, he's helping her learn to walk! So sweet!"

Athena was glad to see her baby brother so happy.

"Sissy, can baby gowal and I go swim n find food?" Dane asked his big sister.

"Hang on a second, I'll go with you, let me see Mitchin off to his meeting." Athena told him

"O.k. we'll wait in the water," the defiant prince told her.

"Well, it looks like you'd better go and keep an eye on the babies... I'll give ya a holler when I get back. You are so beautiful, Athena," he said, then kissed her the kind of kiss that made her knees go weak. Then said, "I love you, too."

Athena just smiled and watched him leave, feeling breathless... she'd never in her life experienced falling in love like that... it was amazing! The only word to describe it was, WOW! Being made love to by an angel was an experience like none other! She had met her match with the angel... She pulled herself back together, then hurried to go catch up to the babies.

Much to her surprise, the feeling stayed with her once she was back in the sea.

———

Chapter 8

"Excuse me, I'm Mitchin, representative of Queen AlaHanDrea. I have an appointment with General Williamson," Mitchin told the male clerk.

The clerk looked him up and down, then pressed a button on his desk and said, "General, there's a man here to see you, says his name is Mitch, representing queen somebody, pulling a wheeled table with a sheet over it."

"The general will see you now," he told Mitchin, then rolled his eyes.

Mitchin rolled his display table into the general's office. "Good morning, General, nice to meet you, I'm Mitchin, here on behalf of Queen AlaHanDrea," he held his hand out for a shake, but the general basically ignored it.

"O.K. you have your minute, let's see what you're going to do with it," the general said, rather pessimistically.

"Yes, well," Mitchin pulled the cover off of the display and went through the entire demonstration.

"Interesting. Very interesting. That's quite an undertaking. So, according to your data, quakes will be lessened.

At least, those tied to volcanic activity, but volcanic eruptions would be eliminated by the channels cut for the controlled flow of lava, as well as the vents, that will retard the buildup of pressure, fascinating.

And you said your name is Mitchin, I'm sorry, I didn't catch your last name."

"It's just Mitchin, where I'm from, we have but one name."

"Interesting, and where is it that you're from that people have but 1 name?" the general asked, sarcasm in his voice.

Mitchin took a deep breath. This was the part he was dreading and hoping to avoid...

"General, there's no easy way to say this, I'm an Angel."

"Excuse me, you're a what" the general asked.

Mitchin took off his jacket and rolled his wings out. "I'm an angel."

The look on the general's face was priceless!

"I'm actually here on vacation.

Here, in the flesh form, that is. You see, there's this woman... Anyway, I'm here on vacation.

Queen AlaHanDrea showed me this system in hopes of saving lives, as well as property. She chose me to bring it to you, so, here I am.

Please know how nervous I am. I'm sure I'm saying things that may challenge your belief system." Mitchin told the skeptical general.

"So, you're an angel. I go to church, young man... From Heaven, I'm guessing. So, if you're an angel, may I speak to you openly?" The general asked.

"Certainly," Mitchin replied.

"Well, it's my grandson. He isn't well." The general began.

"General, pardon me for saying so, but Tommy's biggest problem is his mother and grandmother are smothering him. They inadvertently keep him sick by treating him as though he is sickly and weak." Mitchin explained.

"If you don't mind, put your wings away for a minute, I'm not sure my clerk would understand." He said to Mitchin, then called his clerk into his office, "take these plans down to the Corp of engineers at once. Be sure they get this envelope as well. I will be out of the office for a bit. I'm going home to check on my grandson."

"Yes, General." The clerk said, saluted, then left with the demo table and data envelope.

"Now that he's gone, would you mind terribly accompanying me to my home? I just live about a block from here," the general no sooner said it before he found himself standing in his own front yard. "How'd you do that?" The startled general asked.

"I told you, I'm an angel," Mitchin explained.

"Yes, that you did."

General Williamson's wife, Barbara, was startled when they walked into the kitchen.

"Sorry to have startled you, sweetheart, this is Mitchin. He's come to have a look at Tommy.

Mitchin thinks he may know how to make Tommy get better."

"It's nice to meet you, Mrs. Williamson." Mitchin said as he gently shook her hand.

"It's nice to meet you, too, Mitchin. I was just about to take Tommy his lunch," Barbara told him.

"If you don't mind, I will join you, does Tommy not come out and sit at the table?" Mitchin asked.

"No, his mother and I think it's best he get his rest," she explained.

"Here, let me get the door for you," Mitchin said.

"Thank you. Tommy, I have your lunch and you have a visitor, this is Mitchin. He wants to have a look at you, to see what he can do about making you get better," Tommy's grandmother explained.

"Hi, Tommy, I'm Mitchin, how are you today?"

Tommy sat up on the side of the bed to eat his lunch of soup and crackers with juice.

He was a frail looking boy of 5.

His skin was pale, and he had dark circles under his eyes.

"Well, I guess I will leave you two, then, just call me if you need me," Barbara said, then left the room.

"So, Mitchin, are you a doctor?" Tommy asked.

"Actually, I'm an angel."

"Wow! Really? A real live angel?"

"Yes, I sure am! Ya know that lunch doesn't look very appetizing, how would you like me to get you something more appealing?" Mitchin made a tray with chicken nuggets, Mac n cheese, buttered corn on the cob, a hot roll and a big glass of milk, appear.

"Oh wow! Is all of that for me?" Tommy asked.

"It sure is! Just eat it slowly so you don't get a tummy ache."

"Wow! This is really good!" Tommy said as he chewed his food.

"I'm glad you like it. Tommy, you need to start going outside to play with other children. You need to be out in the fresh air and sunshine. It's not good for you to always be inside."

"I like drawing and learning to read and write and stuff," he protested.

"Well, you can do those things outside," Mitchin told him.

"O.k., fine by me, but mama and granny won't say yes," Tommy commented.

"How about I go talk to them for you? I will be right back. Remember to take your time eating."

"O.k. Mitchin, good luck with momma and granny!"

Mitchin winked at him as he left the room.

"Mrs. Williamson, I've taken the liberty of preparing some menus of food Tommy needs to eat on a daily basis.

Also, he needs to go outside, even if he lays on a lounge, he needs to be outside. Once he gains some strength, he needs to play ball, play with other kids, ride a bike, climb trees and do all the things little boys do. If he doesn't, he will die young. He also needs to be in school. Public school." Mitchin explained.

Barbara started to protest but decided to just let the nice-looking fella just leave.

General Williamson smiled and thanked Mitchin for his visit, promising to let Mitchin know how it went with the Corp of engineers.

Then, he invited Mitchin to please stop by any time, socially.

Mitchin smiled and said his goodbyes.

All in all, he felt the meeting went well.

With all of that behind him, he had a mermaid to go play with... "Wow, she said she loves me," he said out loud to no one... A great big smile stayed on his face all of the way back home.

Chapter 9

AlaHanDrea was sitting on the ground on a blanket, playing with her toes, drool running down her belly, when she heard someone coming towards her.

As it turned out, it was several somebody's. The small group of hunters had wandered into her area.

"Hey Jeff, I found a baby! There must be a mother around here someplace, she looks to be well taken care of!" Justin, the oldest of the small group said.

"Wow, you did find a baby. Look, it has wings! Hi there, little one, where's your mommy?" Jeff asked her.

"Look around, the woman must be around here someplace. She sure is a pretty little thing! With wings like that, we could probably sell her for quite a bit!" He no more had it said than he turned to vapor and was inhaled! AlaHanDrea burped, then said, "Scuse me," and giggled.

Jeff stood there for a moment, in shock, then, he pulled his pistol from its holster, but before he could do anything else, he, too, turned to vapor and was inhaled.

That time, she burped twice, then excused herself and giggled.

The other members of the hunting party met the same fate as their friends...

Most of them fed the baby!

All that was left of them was some gear and a few corpses.

Athena stopped by to check on the baby, when she stumbled over some of the gear the hunters had left behind.

She gathered up the trail of gear that led right to the baby girl.

"AlaHanDrea, did you get visitors this morning?" Athena asked her.

She just nodded her head, yes, looking at the ground.

"Did you make a meal of them?" She asked

Again, the baby looked at the ground and nodded.

"O.k., did they try to hurt you?" Athena asked her.

This time, she looked up at Athena and nodded her head yes. " Da wan seeeeew me fo money."

"They wanted to sell you for money?" Athena asked.

"Uh huh, and shoot me, so I ate dem."

"Well, good girl! Those were bad men!"

"Uh huh, he poooo a gun at me," she said, then sighed.

"Oh, baby girl, well, do you have a full belly?"

"Uh huh,"

"Well, good then," Athena told her.

She reached up for Athena to hold her, so, the substitute mom sat on the ground and put AlaHanDrea on her lap. "AlaHanDrea, I'm going to hold you, but don't you ever try to absorb me, is that clear? You don't ever want to absorb me! Not unless I ask you to! Is that clear?"

"I no asor you Afweena, I wubs my Afweena, weers my Dane? I Sweepy Afweena, I veewy sweepy,"

"Oh, sweet baby girl, you go ahead and go to sleep. I will hold you until you fall asleep, and I will stand guard while you rest. It's ok, go ahead and sleep now..."

The tired baby girl woke up feeling refreshed. Athena didn't notice she was awake at first, she was distracted by the feeling that they were being watched.

She'd been feeling like that since emerging from the sea... Because she Was being watched.

"Look, I know you're out there, why are you afraid to show yourselves? Are you ugly or something?" Athena said to no one in particular.

"We are not afraid of the likes of you, fish girl. And we damned sure are not ugly, bitch!" It was a female warrior, she looked to be tribal...

"O. K, so, you're actually very pretty, just not very bright..." Athena responded with a smirk.

"Why has that kid got a crown on its head, it looks like a real crown," the rude woman asked her.

"Because, she is a queen," Athena told her.

"Well, your queen has drool running down her belly!

We will be taking that crown," the woman told her.

"Oh yeah? Think so, huh? O.k. go ahead, take it from her, she's just a tiny baby, right?" Athena teased.

"Josie, go collect that crown," she ordered. Josie did as she was ordered.

When she reached for AlaHanDrea's crown, the baby showed her fangs for the first time and injected her venom into the would be thief.

"What the... It Bit Me!" Josie said, then screamed out in pain before convulsing, foaming at the mouth, then falling over dead!

Athena had no idea the baby could do that!

"Nice, baby girl, very nice!"

Darts began bouncing backwards about 6 feet before reaching Athena or AlaHanDrea, hitting the babies force fields. Arrows began bouncing off the invisible wall, then spears! AlaHanDrea just laughed.

"Hey fish girl, think you're real smart, don't you?

Give me that crown or die, fish girl!" The woman threatened her.

"Well, if you want that crown, you're going to have to get it yourself, I'm not taking it from her," Athena told her, laughing a little.

The loud-mouthed woman began to levitate! Athena looked over at the baby and she was pointing her tiny finger at the woman. She twirled her finger, and the woman began spinning in the air!

AlahanDrea laughed as she began moving her finger up and down, bouncing the woman off the ground over and over again, then turned her upside down and started bouncing her off of the ground again, laughing and cooing.... Then, she flung her hand sideways, and the woman went flying through the air, bouncing off of a huge tree trunk, unconscious.

The baby girl laughed, clapping her hands.

The other women started to try to charge at them, only to discover they were stuck to the ground in some kind of weird goo.

AlaHanDrea let the force fields down and began crawling over to the women...

Terror filled the intruders as that tiny baby crawled towards them, only to stop and sit up, clapping and laughing.

When the women looked up, they saw what was making the baby laugh with excitement!

Huge Bears walked up on them.

The women watched while one of the bears shifted to human state!

"Well, what have we here? Looks like stupid people to me," Bjorn asked, then said, "hello baby girl, are these bad women bothering you, sweet baby?"

"Uh huh, da arewa. Da tink da wan take my cwown. Da bad. Da tink da kiww Afweeeena an me, too." She told Bjorn.

"Is that right? We will see about that; Leon and William will be here in a minute. Let's see how these ladies like wolves, lions and bears...!" The aggravated king said to the baby girl.

"Good to see you guys. Baby girl needed someone to come take care of her light work!" Athena teased.

"Gentlemen, were y'all aware that she has fangs and venom?" Athena asked.

"Seriously? No, I had no idea. I'm willing to bet that my daughter doesn't know it, either!

She nurses the child, and I don't think she knows. Is that what killed that one over there?" Bjorn asked.

"Ya, that one tried to take baby girls crown," Athena told him.

"Doesn't look to me like she was very successful," Bjorn said with a chuckle.

"Hey y'all, what goes?" Leon said as he walked up the trail into AlaHanDrea's area, with his cub right behind him.

"Well, we actually just got here, but, apparently, these females were trying to rob and kill Princess Athena and Queen AlaHanDrea.

As you can plainly see, it hasn't been going very well for them. They seem to be having a rather bad day," Bjorn's smart aleck nature was more than obvious.

"Looks like it! So, you stupid bitches wanted to murder a baby? Not very bright, are you?" Leon said.

William approached the group. "I heard that. These nasty bitches wanted to murder our baby girl? Stupid, aren't they? They wanted to murder our Athena? Really dumb for pretty women. Baby girl, do we have to kill them right away, or can we play with them first?" William asked.

"You mean pway wit dems wike towies? Kiww dems waita? Kk Da yuwus. Yu had dem. Da yuwus. Had funz." She told him, then made the goo go away.

Electronic collars appeared on the women.

If they did anything wrong, the collars tightened.

If they moved too far away from the group, the collars tightened.

"Very nice, baby girl!" William remarked.

"DUDE, you think that's nice; baby girl has fangs and venom!" Bjorn told him.

"Oh, well, damn! Good to know!" William said.

Leon looked around, then said, "looks to me like we now have a dozen or so, pretty slaves. You guys thinking what I'm thinking?"

"Probably," Bjorn remarked.

William said, "I'll call my pack," then laughed ...

The very next day, a search group of about 30 people came looking for some missing hunters.

Only 1 returned to talk about it and that 1 was in a state of hysteria.

A different search party went looking for the lady warriors.

None returned.

Word of monsters in the wilderness, quickly spread across the human sectors.

When General Williamson heard about it, he got worried about Mitchin and his Queen AlaHanDrea.

If there were monsters in the wilderness, the angel and his queen were in danger!

Hunting parties were formed to go in and find these monsters and destroy them.

None returned.

Larger hunting parties were formed.

None returned, none living, anyway.

A pile of remains were left at the edge of the wilderness.

General Williamson put together some gear, grabbed a Jeep and headed for the wilderness.

He really liked Mitchin.

The information Mitchin brought to them was nothing short of genius!

He felt he owed Mitchin's young queen the protection of the armed forces, if she was being threatened by monsters.

The most important gear he took with him was a small white flag...

The jeep had to be left at the edge of the wilderness, he'd have to hike the rest of the way.

He took a deep breath and began walking ...

The general hadn't travelled far before he was met by a nice-looking young man in incredible physical condition.

"Hello there, I'm General Williamson, I'm looking for Mitchin, the angel, Mitchin."

"Why?" the man asked.

"I have business with him," the general answered.

The young man tilted his head back and hollered out Mitchin's name. A moment later, Mitchin appeared.

"Oh! General Williamson, so nice to see you. What brings you way out here?"

"Actually, I'm concerned about the safety of your young queen.

I've heard stories of hunters, as well as search parties, vanishing, due to monsters in the wilderness.

I'd like to offer your queen the protection of the armed services."

"That's very kind of you. I feel it only fair to tell you that Queen AlaHanDrea is probably one of the most powerful, if not the most powerful creature ever born.

She is nothing short of Amazing! Truthfully, she could protect the armed forces, and she's just a baby."

"What do you mean, she's just a baby?" The General asked him.

"I mean, she is only a few months old."

"Seriously?'

"Ya, seriously! She's still a baby!

Would you like to meet her?" Mitchin asked him.

"Yes, please... I'd love to meet your baby queen. So, what you're telling me, is that a baby told us how to prevent volcanic eruptions... An infant girl....... Told the Corp of engineers, how to prevent volcanic........

And they heard her?

Well, of course they heard her, she sent an angel to tell them!

Oh, this gets better with every passing moment..." the general said with a touch of humorous sarcasm in his voice.

"It is kind of funny when you think about it, general," Mitchin said with a chuckle.

"Yeah, it's freaking hilarious!" General Williamson replied.

Mitchin took the general by the hand ... a moment later they were standing in front of AlaHanDrea.

She was sitting on the ground on a blanket. When she saw Mitchin, she got all excited and started bouncing on her butt, clapping her little hands and laughing. "Hello, baby girl. I'm glad to see you, too! This is General Williamson; he came to meet you in person. He loves your ideas about the volcanos," Mitchin told her.

"Hewwo Genewal, nice to mee you," Alahandrea said.

Surprised at how well such a tiny baby could speak, the General sat down on the ground and said, "it's very nice to meet you, too, sweetie. You're very pretty, as well as smart.

I would love to be your friend......If, you would like that, too."

"Uh, huh, you nice man. You gotta mommy n babay, too? Can you see da faces in you hed?"

The generals' family appeared, looking startled. He quickly explained things to his wife, daughter and grandson.

Tommy was really excited about being there, as well as the magic.

They no sooner began to get comfortable, than a quake began shaking the ground they were standing on!

Chapter 10

Creatures scattered, trying to locate and rescue as many as they could from the rockslides, caused by the ground moving like it did.

Fortunately, the quake was only moderately strong, causing minimal damage.

Of course, if you were one of the ones in the 'Minimal' count, it didn't seem so minimal!

The quakes were coming larger and with more frequency.

Zinith 6 was the planet that Ion 6 was moon to.

Zinith 6 was also home to The Watchers, an ancient race of super beings, responsible for relocating deserving species from doomed planets, to planets capable of not only sustaining them, but allowing them to flourish, as well as advance. Once relocated, the watchers would consume the doomed planet.

The race had occupied Zinith 6 for more millenniums than they could count, which most likely led to their being a bit complacent.

They had gotten used to remaining in the galaxy for their food, given there were trillions of trillions of stars with planets in their orbits.

With food so plentiful at home, so to speak, they had gotten used to "staying home" for supper.

Had the race of super beings been traveling outside of their Galaxy, as they had done in times gone by, they would have seen the changes in steering currents that changed the directions that the Galaxies of the region traveled... They would have noticed the neighboring Galaxy that had changed course, causing it to be directly in the path of the Galaxy containing Zinith 6...

2 Galaxies that were then on a collision course... a collision that would cause both Galaxies to be ripped apart, slinging stars out in the vastness of space, causing others to supernova, destroying all life on the planets orbiting them, in both scenarios.

Curiosity as to the reason for the seasons; for the unusual weather events & seismic activities, had the watchers sending scouts out into the galaxy to see what they could discover.

When the scouts returned, it was with news of massive disruptions in the flow throughout the entire Galaxy, with no obvious reason as to why.

Something had very definitely changed the flow of the entire galaxy ......

But what?

It remained a mystery ...

But only for a short while...

Babygirl began playing with her hands; she'd make 2 fists, then hold her little hands out and make her tiny fists smash together, then making blow up sounds...

Then she'd say, "Mistow Jax!" Then, she'd do it again and say, "Mistow Jax!" She was referring to Prince Harmon, nickname, Mr. Jax, heir to the throne of the watchers.

First officer for species relocations...

Mitchin stood, watching her, listening, trying to understand what she was trying to tell them.

A chill shook him, when he saw AlaHanDrea's thoughts and saw the destruction of their worlds!

He didn't quite know what to think. But he was an angel, and it wasn't his news to tell.

Mitchin's faith was with God, whom he trusted to keep him safe.

His attitude was, "what will be, will be."

Mitchin wasn't on Ion 6 to change destiny, he was on vacation. It wasn't for him to interfere with destiny.

Knowing that Mitchin understood her, was calming to the baby girl... It was 'enough for now'.

For the moment, all of their attention needed to be on what was happening right that moment... Rebuilding... Rescuing...

Surviving as the quakes worsened...

Their moon was beginning to have nearly daily quakes, some so small they could barely be felt and others, so strong, structures collapsed, the ground shifted and cracked open... Lives were lost...

Volcanoes began erupting.

The Corp of engineers worked feverishly to cut vent holes with lava troughs into the volcanos to relieve the pressure inside of the moon... The quakes and eruptions were causing quite a bit of chaos.

In spite of the chaotic atmosphere, Alahandrea was growing rather quickly, as most babies do...

The "growing ever more powerful babygirl" finally decided it was time to assist the Corp of engineers; they worked entirely too slowly for her taste.

The tiny girl was shocked when she was unable to cut through layers of cooled lava flow.

But then, she was barely a toddler!

The Girl was technically, still a Baby!

General Williamson and his family were sure glad to be with the baby queen when the quakes began. Their home was completely buried under tons of rock, dirt and debris.

Assumed to have been home at the time of the quake, the entire family was counted as dead by base officials.

No one felt compelled to correct them.

"General, I didn't guess you to be a rebel, I suppose we should be preparing a home for your family that won't fall over when the ground moves," Prince William V told him. Then said, "doesn't any of your family know your truth?"

The General looked at him for a moment, then said, "No, how Did You know?"

"We know our own, General;

You weren't raised around your own kind, why not?" William asked.

The General thought for a moment, then said,

"My family was killed. I was shifted to human state by my mother, when trouble broke out. When I was discovered, they thought I was human. No one ever knew my truth.

My wife and I adopted our daughter, no, my wife does not know.

I don't shift anymore. I haven't shifted since the day my family was murdered.

I've lived as a human... and I suppose I will remain a human."

"Have you forgotten your magic as well?" William asked.

"Ya, I suppose I have at that..."

"You need to find you again, General!" William told the man.

"You're right about that, for sure!" The general couldn't help but to agree.

"Here, General, come with me for a minute... O.K., there's no one around, go ahead, do it, shift, but do it quickly so you're not discovered."

"Why do you want me to....." He was interrupted by William.

"I am the future king of your kind, I am Prince William the 5th, now, I said, Shift!"

A moment later, a beautiful, huge, muscular white, silver and black markings, white wolf stood before William. "See, now that wasn't so hard, was it?

General, look me in the eyes, and remain shifted, please, look at me... It's your eyes, your markings... General... Look, follow me, I will just have to show you.

Try to keep up, will ya?

Now come-on!" William said, as he took off running, with the General hot on his heels.

They ran, jumping from boulder to Boulder, jumping over small bushes, under growth. etc... stuff...

It had been decades since the General last felt himself in his true k9 form, decades since he had felt the ground beneath his paws and the wind in his fur as he ran through the wilderness of Ion 6... Decades since he had felt himself as he truly was!

He felt reborn!

They ran until they reached the central pack.

When they entered the packs area, everyone just froze, staring at the General!

They all looked as though they'd seen a ghost!

"William, son, you've found him! You've found him! You've found Prince Kai!

Bless the powers that be, son, you found him!!!

He's alive and you found him!!!" Cheers and applause rose up from the pack!!! Everyone gathered around the General, looking at him, sniffing him, in utter disbelief that he was really there with them.

"Father, in his other form, He is known as The General!

He's lived as a human since the day his family was murdered!

William the 4th, looked him in the eyes and said, "You really don't remember who you are, do you? Well, I'm not surprised that you rose to general status as a human.

You're my nephew, boy! Your daddy was my brother! My litter mate brother! You've been missing for more than 40 years. We found the bodies of your parents and siblings, but never knew what became of you.

Welcome home, boy, welcome home!"

William V wasted no time in calling AlaHanDrea to tell her the awesome news and to thank her for her role in bringing his cousin back home to where he belonged.

Now all they had to do was to tell the Generals wife, daughter and grandson!

Now that was going to be an interesting discussion!

"I remember some, I remember the murders. I also remember that Unger Wolf betrayed my parents and delivered them to their enemies for slaughter.

That's why I never tried to return. I was afraid and didn't know who could be trusted.

I had forgotten who I was for ages. I thought my memories were just dreams... But then, I met this angel, Mitchin, he just walked into my office one day, and it all began to come back to me.

I still thought I had dreamed it all.

Then, I came looking for Mitchin and just being in the danger of the wilderness, well, memories have been flooding back to me!

I have a headache from it all.

I remember the pack!

I DO remember y'all!

Maybe not perfectly, but I do remember y'all! I do remember y'all. I do remember y'all... I do remember........ The General tilted his head back and howled as loudly and as long as his lungs would allow!

The pack returned his howl!

Then everyone began laughing, howling, hugging the General, welcoming him home.

Kai's uncle said, "Your father and I were litter mates! We never knew what happened to you! We found what remained of the battle scene, but found no sign of you. We thought you were lost forever.

Wow!

It's so good to have you home!

Wow!"

"Really, Uncle? I find that very hard to believe. You see, I was hiding in a tiny dug out at the side of a small hill, covered by bushes. I was there, I saw your face, I heard your voice...

You ordered the slaughter of my entire family!

It was you!

I'm sure of it now, hearing your voice again!

It was the only way you'd get the throne!

You had my family murdered and blamed it on the humans!

That's why I never returned! I didn't know who to trust and I was too young to figure it all out!

Well, I'm no longer a child, uncle, and I was there! I heard you with my own ears! I also saw you slaughter most of the wolves that killed my family!" Kai said, growling at his uncle... He wasn't alone! The entire pack was growling and surrounding the king...

"Hold him right here, I know how to get the truth! I will be right back!" Prince William instructed, then took off like the wind.

"AlaHanDrea! AlaHanDrea! Please, come quick! Jump on my back, please, we need you, it's urgent!" Prince William hollered.

"We need fast? See where we go in you head," she instructed while sitting on his back. A moment later, they were back at wolf camp.

"Nice trick! Baby girl, we need to know the truth. Can you please retrieve Kai's memory and show everyone? From when he was a pup?" William asked her.

"Sure, I wike you as a woofs Genewal... Hole stiwww.....

A viewing screen appeared.

Prince William said, "we want the day his family was killed."

"Pwease focus dat day, Genewal," AlaHanDrea told him.

Memories of that horrible day began to play on the screen.

The pack watched while their beloved royal family were slaughtered senselessly. They watched as the terrified queen shifted her baby boy then hid him just before she was murdered by misguided pack outlaws.

They listened to King William instructing others, then watched while he killed most of the wolves that had assisted him in killing his brother, taking his brothers crown and giving it to him.

Only 2 of the loyal wolves helping William remained. The pack listened to their king's own brother instructing those 2 to find Kai and make sure he was dead!

They were horrified as well as beyond furious!

No wonder Kai had been terrified to return!

AlaHanDrea pointed her finger at William IV and raised him off the ground, suspending him in the air for all to see, she also shifted him to man state. She felt it would be much easier to do what needed to be done...

She was right...

The other two wolves were rounded up.

The baby queen suspended them on either side of their leader.

"Thank you, baby girl. Please leave them up there for a while, we need to hold court and decide what needs to be done," William V said to her.

"O.K. I go, dis fo youse to do, bye bye." She said just before vanishing.

She returned shortly after, lowered the murderers and turned them to living statutes. "Pwobwem swowved. Da awibe bu not awibe... ded bu not ded... da wiw suffa, ok bye bye now, no mo pwobwem bye bye" and she was gone.

William V said, "O.K. well ya, O.K. I suppose that IS a solution!

Prince Kai had a crown placed on his head... The crown of a prince. The king's crown was placed on William in accordance with pack law. Kai needed time to adjust before being placed as ruler, then he and William would rule together.

It was both a time of sorrow and a time of celebration.

The next step was breaking the news to Kai's wife and kids.

Overall, they took the news pretty good. His wife was comforted by the fact that there was no reason to continue keeping her own secret.

She prepared a special evening for the family and invited AlaHanDrea, wolves, dragons, lions, bears, Athena... Mitchin...

She stood up before all of her guests and said, "Thank you all for coming and welcome. So much has changed in such little time... So many adjustments for so many... There's no easy way to say this, so, I will just have to show y'all.

Ya know, we all have our little secrets, even me! All secrets must eventually be revealed, so... Gosh, I'm so nervous! O.K. so, here I go!"

A moment later, a gorgeous, giant, golden, winged Cougar stood before them!

Total silence from her guests...

Jaws dropped!

Kai didn't know quite what to say! He was married to a cougar!

A kitty cat!

But wolves are dogs!

Cougars are cats!

They both cracked up laughing......as did all of their guests!

Chapter 11

AlaHanDrea's second birthday celebration was an all-day party. Dane showed up with some very nice gifts from the sea for his little girlfriend.

They were actually celebrating their 1 1/2-year anniversary as boyfriend and girlfriend.

The array of sea shells in intricately hand woven baskets, was nothing short of breathtaking! She absolutely loved her seashells and was amazed that there were more gifts...

Dane sat the next gift box down in front of her, looking suspiciously like the cat that ate the canary.

Unwrapping the box revealed the most beautiful little music box, jewelry box. Dane wound it for her, using the built in box key, then turned it towards her, opening the lid to reveal a tiny ballet dancer, dancing in circles as the music played.

AlaHanDrea loved it so much, she wasn't noticing all of the jewelry the box contained. Not at first, anyway. All of the pieces were simple and pretty, very appropriate for a baby queen.

Dane further surprised her when he took a microphone and stepped up onto a stage he magically created.

"Hello everyone! Welcome to my girlfriends birthday party! Thanks for coming to join us in celebrating the life of this incredible baby girl...

I have one more gift to give... I wrote this myself and I want a sing it for y'all now..."

(Prince Dane wrote her the cutest song for her birthday...)

~~When a boy loves a girl, the right way a boy loves a girl, the girl that loves the boy that loves her, all is right in the world and we are so happy together....and when we are grown, and out on our own, when I'm a man and you're a woman, I will love you the way a man loves a woman, the way I love the woman that's in love with the man that's in love with her, and that's me...I'm sure you can plainly see, that's me... And when we grow old, our stories will be told, the stories of a boy that was in love with a girl, the way a boy loves a girl, the way this boy loves this girl who is in love with the boy that loves her... And until then, while we are still so young, I love you the way a boy is supposed to love the girl that's in love with the boy that's in love with the girl that loves him and he ... is me...~~~

Aaaww could be heard in unison, then everyone stood and applauded the young prince's gift to his baby girlfriend. 2 and 4 years old and obviously devoted to one another, already!

Prince Dane and Queen AlaHanDrea were the Love Story everyone got to watch grow up. Romancing one another from the cradle...

Dane excused himself to go relieve himself.

AlaHanDrea was surrounded by royalty and royal guard giving her gifts.

She opened the last gift and wanted to show Dane, but he still had not returned. Tommy said, "I'll go get him, your majesty," and took off in the same direction Dane had gone in. About 15 minutes had passed, but neither boy returned!

Athena began to really get worried, so AlaHanDrea summoned them both!

No response ...

She called out their names, demanding they both appear before her, but, again, no response.

The worry just got real!

Athena was in a near panic, screaming out for her father!

Kind Neptune wasted no time in popping up to find out what was making his daughter hysterical. He ordered the guards to find Dane right away! And Tommy, too! He summoned the Mers...

They obeyed without question and an all-out search began for the 2 missing boys. One of the guards called out that they had found something, one of Tommy's shoes and signs of a struggle! Then, they found Dane's gold necklace! The one AlaHanDrea had given him the day they met! He NEVER took it off, yet it lay on the ground...

Neptune was beside himself!

Viewing screens appeared high in the sky, huge screens, where everyone could see and hear the broadcast. It was a plea for the return of the two boys.

A short time later, someone, a masked someone, came on the screen.

It was the kidnappers!

Leon, William and Bjorn stood by King Neptune as they listened to the demands of the kidnappers.

Deliver AlaHanDrea's head on a platter, or receive Dane and Tommy's heads on the platter!

The choice was all theirs to make!

The Generals family was beside themselves!

The General knew they couldn't ever make a deal with kidnappers!

Not for anyone at Any time!

It went against everything they believed in to negotiate with kidnappers...

Still, it was Dane and Tommy!

AlaHanDrea made herself invisible. She knew she'd sure miss those boys, but she had no intention of dying, or allowing anyone else to try to make her dead!

It was truly unfortunate that the boys would lose their lives.

She was trying her best to figure out how to handle the situation, but Leon, Bjorn, William and Neptune were already on the situation!

They produced a fake head on a platter to go get the boys back...and, it worked!

By the time the kidnappers realized the head was fake, the boys were back safe and sound with their families. AlaHanDrea remained invisible for a while, but no one came looking for her, so, she materialized .

Still, Athena didn't come, the general didn't come, Neptune didn't come... None of the Mers came... More than a weak had passed and not even Mitchin had seen Athena, Dane, Neptune or any of the Mers, for that matter. AlaHanDrea tried summoning all of them, no one replied.

Every day, AlaHanDrea and Mitchin both, set out to try to find and reach any mer. But, it appeared as though all of the Mers had up and moved away!

AlaHanDrea became very depressed. She decided that king Neptune was so upset about Danes kidnapping, that to keep him safe, he took all of them far away from her.

She missed Athena the most!

She wasn't one to cry, at least, until then. She shed tears daily for her missing friends.

She found it hard to believe they'd all just up and leave like that without even saying goodbye!

Yet, every single one of them were gone!

Gone without a trace....

Mitchin was an angel and he couldn't even find them!

Depression had set in.

She went out every day, swimming, looking for any sign of where the Mers went.

A couple of months had passed when an alien ship was detected in the outer atmosphere.

King Leon hunted AlaHanDrea down until he finally found where she was hiding out, alone, crying most of the time.

Heartbroken and alone, the baby girl looked terrible!

Her will to continue living was obviously dwindling by the hour.

She barely even responded when she saw Leon.

"There you are baby girl! We've all been searching for you for quite some time. Look, baby girl, I'm real sorry about your mers, but, baby girl, the rest of us need you and we need you badly right now!

There's an alien ship in the outer atmosphere and they don't look to be friendly.

Not at all!

AlaHanDrea, life comes with pain. I'm sorry, but it just does!

Grief is a natural part of life. But you can't quit! The rest of us still love you and need you!"

"They wouldn't even let me see Dane or Tommy, either one, once they were free! Athena snatched Danes hand and took him away! She said it was too dangerous for him to be around me anymore.

I am a liability they don't want for Dane.

They wouldn't even let me see him! Or Tommy!"

Tears were rolling down her cheeks.

I wove my Afweena, Weon. She wike my mama. She my best fweind... She hold me, wock me, sing to me... Now, she hates me!"

Her boohoos became very loud with hard sobbing... I so mad wif her, Weon! She take my Dane away fwom me! Wahh hah hah, she cried.

"Yes, she sure did, and there's not one thing you can do about it!

King Neptune has the right to try to protect his children, whether we agree or not!

I know, it really sucks!

Look, how's about you come with me and kill some aliens, it'll make you feel much better!" Leon coaxed.

"These aliens are as much of a threat to the mer population as they are to the rest of the moon! Show king Neptune that he's wrong to keep you away from your Dane! Protect them, even though they are being mean to you, by over protecting Dane!

Show them how much they need you!

Protect them, don't allow the aliens to kill them! Please baby girl, we can fight them without you, but we'd loose far less lives, with you! Come on, baby girl, come fight with me!

Ride on my neck and I will fly you into battle myself personally! " Leon pleaded.

"You wight, Weon. O.k. but, I weak & hungwy."

"I thought you might be, foods right outside, waiting for you..."

AlaHanDrea wasn't very nice to her food!

She slowly absorbed the first one, pulling him inside of herself, he went in feet first and appeared to be sticking out of her side! Slowly sinking deeper inside, screaming, unable to thrash about, slipping ever so slowly into her until he completely disappeared! AlaHanDrea burped, passed gas, then giggled, saying "Scuse me!"

The second one, she made his arms and legs fall off, causing him to scream hysterically, then turned him to vapor to be inhaled.

By the third one, she must have been getting tired, because the rest she vaporized and inhaled them.

Sleep came quickly after such a large, needed meal. Leon patiently waited by her side.

Finally, she woke up, ate again and went back to sleep. It would be the following day & 3 more meals, before she would be fit for any kind of activity.

Leon had been prepared to have to strengthen her. He wasn't a bit surprised at the time it took...

The alien ship made no attempts to communicate, it just hung there, orbiting Ion 6.

AlaHanDrea finally woke up, went for a swim and checked out an area she loved to visit, by a huge rockslide under the sea, but saw nothing to indicate where the Mers might be.

Then, something caught her eye. It was Athena's bracelet! She was sure of it and it was wedged under a rock! Athena had been right there and lost it! She put the bracelet on and swam for Leon to show it to him.

Mitchin popped up by Leon. " How's baby girl today?" Mitchin asked.

"She's swimming."

"Weon! Weon! Woook what I Found! I tink is Afweenas! Wook! Mitchin!!! Mitchin, wook, isn't dis Afweens's bwacewet?" The anxious child asked?

"Well, let me see it? Yes, I do believe this is Athena's...

She never takes it off, where did you find this?"

"Under some woks by de piwe of woks dat swided..."

Just then, they heard a huge explosion!

They looked up and saw a pillar of smoke billowing up into the air near a settlement...

Leon shifted, AlaHanDrea jumped on and they were off to investigate!

Mitchin headed for the source of the smoke.

As they suspected, the alien ship was opening fire on the surface of their moon!

AlaHanDrea wasted no time in creating shields to protect the ground, while putting up viewing screens to attempt to communicate.

It didn't take very long for the aliens to respond.

They were very rude to AlahanDrea, so, the temperature inside their ship began to rise. Then, their ship began to shake. The aliens became even more hostile!

Anger filled the 2 ½ year old warrior, as the aliens continued to be violent.

The screams of the aliens could be heard planet wide, over the viewing screens, as the temp inside their ship began baking them alive!

The aliens were literally cooking inside of the mother ship!

Leon quickly returned to the surface to join Bjorn and William.

They no sooner landed, than Leon was placing his hand over Bjorn's and Williams, to combine power!

They began to shoot a beam at the mother ship! AlaHanDrea ran over and placed her hand on top of Leon's!

The beam was magnified!

Suddenly, an enormously powerful beam shot up, engulfing the ship and blew the violent aliens ship into space dust!

The 3 Kings couldn't believe how much power surged through them when the baby girl put her hand in the mix!

Each of them took turns hugging her and spinning her around!

"That was Amazing! Incredible! Wow! Wow! Wow!" William exclaimed.

"Dayum!" Bjorn added.

"Ya, what they said... Wow, AlaHanDrea, thanks! Baby girl, that was Amazing!

"We bwewed dems up!" The baby power house said.

"Yes, we sure did!" Bjorn agreed.

"I only wish we knew more about them" Leon complained.

Mitchin had already gone under the sea. AlaHanDrea went looking for him. It didn't take her very long to locate him. She assumed he went to where she had found that bracelet and she was right.

Mitchin found a few more clues and insisted that AlaHanDrea return to the surface to stay with Bjorn, William and Leon.

A few minutes later, Mitchin surfaced and sat them all down for a quick talk.

"Guys, I found the Mers. Baby girl has been right All along. They did not leave without saying goodbye. Now, AlaHanDrea, I want you to listen to me and listen good! You are to stay here and let Leon, William, Bjorn and I handle this!

I'm powerful like you are, young lady and we can do this!

If you go with us, mers will be put to death, starting with

Neptune and Athena, are you listening to me?

Their lives depend on you staying away. They have been taken captive, but are actually being treated very well. But, as soon as you show up, they will begin killing Mers to force you to kill yourself to stop the executions.

Another thing, sweet baby girl, I don't quite know how to tell you this, but Dane stood up and fought against them!

He tried with all of his might to protect his big sister!

Baby girl, Dane was a hero. I'm so sorry baby girl, but Dane was ..."

"No! No! No! No!

Don't say it! It isn't twue!

If you don't say it, it's not twue!

No, don't say it!!!!! Noooooo!!!!" She screamed.... Lions, tigers, bears and wolves, fairies eagles and owls, unicorns and horses, all came running to console the distraught baby girl, while the men gathered their troops and went after the Mers!

It was time to kick some serious ass!

Mitchin led the pack! On the way to rescue the Mers, an army of Angels joined Mitchin in the front row!

They became an army led by Holy Angels!

There would be no negotiations!

The army was there to free the Mers and that's exactly what they did!

That army was constructed of creatures of magic and was led by an army of Angels!

Intimidating was a huge understatement!

They received little resistance, releasing the entire population of Mers after the first show of combined power!

The angels remained, while the Mers were escorted safely back home to familiar waters.

The Angels made certain nothing like that would ever happen again! They also made sure the humans believed in Angels before they left!

They made sure the humans not only believed in them, but understood And respected the power of Angels before they left!

That day, they instilled unshakable faith in their existence and erased all doubt!

Chapter 12

As thrilled as AlaHanDrea was about the Mers being freed, she was beside herself with grief over Dane.

She just refused to believe that he was gone!

The baby queen was convinced she'd have known it if he'd of passed.

She kept hanging out by that huge pile of rocks.

One day, she got all in a fury and summoned King Neptune.

"It's Dane! Dane is Awive! Dane is Awive! But, not fo Wong if we done huwwy! Hep me moob de woks, pwease hep me moob de woks!

He out of food, he come to me in my dweeam ... he wiw die soon, pwease hep me moob de wocks," she cried. "Dane twapped n food aawww gone! He die soon, oh Pwease hep moob de woks! He in a pocket in der!" She cried!

King Neptune didn't argue with her, he just stood back and pointed his trident at that pile and began blasting it!

Then, he summoned the mers and everyone began moving that pile as quickly as they could!

Baby girl was blasting as hard as she could, right along side King Neptune. She finally stopped, then asked king Neptune if she could please get on his back. He agreed not realizing what would happen when she rolled up in his hair.

He shot straight up with his eyes open wide, as power surged through his veins!

He swelled in size, as well as strength!

His blasting became way more powerful and in very little time, they had managed to blast a small hole through the cooled lava wall that laid behind all of the fallen rocks.

AlaHanDrea uncurled from king Neptune, jumped down from his back, shrank herself in size and swam through the hole they had blasted.

Dane was laying on the floor, looking as though he had already passed away. "DANE!" she screamed! "Oh, Dane! My Dane! I found him! I found Dane! I Found Dane! Stop Bwasting, We comin Out!"

AlaHanDrea shrank Dane to about 6 inches, just like she was, then grabbed his hand and pulled him through the hole. The second they were through the hole, she grew him back to normal size, shaking him, begging him to wake up. King Neptune took Danes lifeless body in his arms... Tears were streaming down the distraught kings face... Mitchin rushed to their side and gently blew air up Danes nostrils.

There was no response. Mitchin did it again, but, still no response.

He took Dane in his arms and did it one more time. That time, Dane began turning his head and coughing!

Dane was ALIVE!

Athena ran over to AlaHanDrea and hugged her, thanking her for saving her little baby brother. Her father wasn't feeling quite so generous.

Mitchin stepped over and asked King Neptune if he was grateful that AlaHanDrea had found Dane... King Neptune looked at Mitchin and said, "I'm thankful that my son has been found, and that you restored his life, But, gratitude towards that little girl? I think Not! It's her fault all of this happened in the first place!

How do I feel gratitude towards that child when My people and I have suffered so? My son was entombed! Alone!

My Nation was kidnapped under the threat of death!

Used as pawns in an attempt to destroy that child!"

"Really?

That's how you see things?

You yourself have enemies because of your great power! Someone's always plotting against you, King Neptune! How many ships have you sank in retaliation? How many innocent bystanders have lost their lives, because you exacted revenge against someone?

That baby girl is Not responsible for any of this! Those who are trying to kill her, also try to kill you and for the same reasons! She didn't ask them to do any of this! She is an innocent victim who just spent months in deep grief over all of this!

She is not responsible for those who hate her for being who and what she is.

You and her are not so different. She has suffered so much! And, you seem to forget, she's only two years old! Almost 3, but still a baby girl and she has suffered more than any child should ever have to.

She loves you, Neptune. Be glad that she does, too.

Getting and remaining close to her is extremely wise. You don't know what the future holds, but I do, and I'm telling you, ol boy, be very glad that she loves you! You really need to get your head right about her, and quickly, too!"

"I suppose you're right, Mitchin. I need to remember that the enemy of my enemy is my friend. Her and I both need to let those who appose us know, that if you mess with one of us, you mess with all of us!

We need to make them fear coming at us again!

We need to plan a strike. We need to strike hard and strike fast, doing as much damage as we can, until they beg for mercy and are to terrified to try something like this in the future... We need to hit em and hit them hard!!!"

"That's not really what I meant."

"Maybe not, but it's what her and I need to do! When that child wrapped herself up in my hair, the power that surged through me was unbelievable! I do believe that together, we are unstoppable! "

Mitchin just looked at him for a moment, then said, "AlaHanDrea, by herself, is unstoppable! She doesn't need you, it's you that needs her!

As a Baby, she is unstoppable.

Imagine her as an adult! Don't you want her on your side? I know that I do!

So does God!

Anybody with any sense wants her as a friend... And lucky you! She sees you as family...

The Sea God had to think about that for a moment.

"It's hard to believe that a toddler holds so much power!

But then, that's why the humans have done what they have done.

Mitchin, the humans have some new weaponry. Scary, bad stuff that repels magic.

They used it against us!

Dane was holding them off really well. Killed a whole bunch of them before they shot him with some kind of transparent bubble that encased him and imprisoned him before the quake caused that landslide. If it works against baby girl...."

"Hmmm, sounds like a job for the General! The humans don't know that he's a wolf." Mitchin replied.

King Neptune looked at Mitchin with a confused look on his face, "Seriously? The General is a wolf?"

"Not just A wolf, he is the missing Prince Kai, if you can believe that!" Mitchin explained.

"Well good for King William! He got his Nephew back! Small consultation for the loss of his brother and the rest of the lost royals, but good for William... And good for the General.

Ya, our side has a General among the humans... Right On!" King Neptune felt much better about things after finding out about the General being Prince Kia.

The news calmed him down a lot.

He went over to AlaHanDrea and gave her a big hug, thanking her for finding Dane, and for Dane still being alive. "Baby girl, I'm so sorry for all of your suffering and heartbreak.

We can all begin to heal now that everyone is free. Try not to worry, your enemies are my enemies, too. We are in this thing together, you and I and we will be victorious! The humans are no match for us, baby girl, not even a little bit!"

AlaHanDrea hugged him, then broke down crying. He held her in his arms, then quickly set her down before they both forgot and she tried to absorb him.

He didn't want to have to kill her and didn't want to die, either. He patted her back to comfort her. She was so worn out, both physically and emotionally, that she fell fast asleep.

———————————

Chapter 13

Returning to base wasn't easy for Prince Kai, aka the General. He pretended that his family was buried alive during the quake and he was trapped, having to dig his way out.

They gave him a medal and a new office.

Pretending to have a vendetta towards the monsters in the wilderness was very difficult, but he was real convincing.

It took no time at all for Prince Kai to be appointed to the new weapons development division, exactly where he wanted to be!

Coming back from the dead, so to speak, showed him exactly who was loyal to him. Hopefully, he'd be able to expand that group.

The more soldiers he could recruit to his side, the better off they would all be. The General really didn't want to have to kill any more than absolutely necessary.

Barbara, their daughter, Tristin and grandson, Tommy, remained back at their home, with the other monsters, in the wilderness.

Barbara and the kids took the news about Kai better than expected, actually.

Barbara seemed relieved. She said that she always knew that he had a secret and had hoped that someday he'd feel compelled to share, but she would have never guessed in a million years just what that secret was.

She really didn't know how to feel about it all, but, she had to admit, they had been more welcomed, treated with more respect and more cared for than they ever were in the human sectors.

Being a general was special, but nothing like her husband being royalty, especially long time missing, newly found royalty!

Now the wife of a shape shifting K9, Barbara was going through a ton of emotional changes.

She found that Kai being a wolf was actually strangely erotic! Of course, he wouldn't be able to come home much while working under cover.

That just meant they treasured the moments he could make it back without raising suspicion.

Much to Barbara's delight, there were more than a few human brides in the community of shape shifting beasts...

Plenty of women to talk with and help with the adjustments.

She was used to the human females, relating to them better than others...

Before arriving in the wilderness, Barbara had no idea there was such a wide variety of shape shifting beasts.

She really only knew of her own kind..

The human communities didn't know about it at all. Oh, there were a few humans in the know, but no one believed them.

The General wasted no time in filling the creatures in on how the weapons against magic worked.

In almost no time at all, they were able to discover ways to neutralize the weapons.

Now that they were aware of the type of technology the humans were developing, they were able to get ahead of the human developers in ways to neutralize the newly developed weaponry.

Once the mission was fulfilled, the beasts staged an accident in the wilderness that caused the General to have appeared to have been captured.

They really didn't want to burn him, they needed him to return.

His loyal troops were captured during the staged accident, as well and taken to an island in the wilderness.

With no way off of the island, the troops were set free. No cages, no shackles, no restraints of any kind.

Row boats sat tied to the doc, unsecured.

Rogle stood as main guard. He was part of the wolves royal guard.

"If I may have your attention please!" Rogle said, trying to get everyone to pay attention.

"You weren't actually captured and may leave when ever you wish.

You were brought here for a private and secure conversation.

This is a place where you can relax, take time to gather your thoughts, etc ... Because, what you're about to hear, may be a bit hard for you to get right away.

The General requested you be brought here.

He considers you all to be friends, or, of like minds and believes you to be able to see the truth in the one sided war against the peace loving beasts of the wilderness.

The struggle is real and has been real for so long, that beasts had to develop a defense mechanism, to prevent being slaughtered into extinction.

It's time you know the full truth..."

Rogle stood and shifted right in front of them! He very quickly shifted back to human form. "Yes, Gentlemen and lady, I, in reality, am a wolf, yet stand before you, as a man."

Stunned silence... Jaws dropped... No one knew quite how to respond to what they had just seen.

Rogle thought it best to just changed the subject all together.

He called for the ladies to begin serving food. They put on a luau type feast, right on the beach......

Complete with dancers, both fire dancers and hula dancers.

A bon fire was lit and glasses were filled with liquor.

It was time to celebrate just being alive.

The music suddenly stopped, when bears and lions come walking out of the tree line, but they transformed into human form on the way to the fire and the music started back up.

Welcome to our world, was said more than once to the troops.

They were asked to please take time to get to know the creatures before passing judgment... they wanted the fighting and the killing to stop.

Their only desire was for the humans to understand that the senseless slaughter of their kind needed to end, preferably without war.

The entertaining of the troops went on for 3 days and nights. At the end of that three days, all of the troops were loyal, as they put it, to life and the freedom to live.

The general did not reveal himself as being Prince Kai to his troops, all he would admit to, was being sympathetic to the beasts and against the senseless slaughter of them.

The General and his troops concocted a story about how they escaped their captors and made it back to base.

The General had them permanently assigned to patrolling the wilderness for the monsters. They were in charge of security between the beasts and the humans, right exactly where they needed to be... to keep the peace. After all, they were the only group to come back out alive and in one piece.

General Williamson just didn't think it was a real good idea for the troops to think they were being led by a beast, rather than by a human, sympathetic to the beasts. At least for a while.

Some of the loyal troops, loyal to the general, as well as the beasts, were stationed in research and development over the weapons, while the rest of them stayed in patrol of the wilderness.

Barbara was thrilled that she got to see more of her husband and loved the turn their lives had taken.

The troops fell in love with the beast communities. The more they got to know the creatures, the more respect they had for the entire community of shape shifters.

More to the point, they fell in love with the baby queen! They came to realize that she was the glue that bound them all to one another.

She amazed them!

Prior to their arriving on the island that changed all of their opinions and lives, the men and women of the armed services weren't even sure they believed magic existed, much less shape shifting.

Once all of their eyes were opened, they were able to see the truth.

There was no respect for the beasts in the human communities. They blamed a lack of education on the subject, and, truthfully, they nailed it!

As time progressed, more and more soldiers shifted over to the 'new armed forces'... The armed forces for all, not just humans... Led by General Williamson... Prince Kai, cousin of William...

AlaHanDrea was swimming with Dane when they heard the sirens go off! She returned to the surface, instructing Dane to take cover and wait for her in a place of safety.

It was another one of the alien ships, like the one that had hung out in the outer atmosphere before opening fire on them... causing them to blow it to pieces.

The tiny queen used her powers to pop over to Leon. He was already waiting for her.

The human soldiers weren't real certain what they should do, or, how they could even do anything against such a threat.

They watched as the creatures capable of flight fell in line behind Leon ... with a toddler on his back!

The precious little girl rolled up in Leon's mane. The Soldiers watched as he swelled in size and took to the skies.

The soldiers were instructed to take cover until such time as alien forces arrived on the ground, if they arrived on the ground.

Jet planes were also in the air. The human Air Force was trying its best.

The baby queen threw forcefields up to protect the jets, barely in time to thwart the beams being shot at them.

The pilots were in complete disbelief when they witnessed the beams Ricocheting off of the force field put up to protect them!

AlaHanDrea was furious over the aliens attempt to destroy the jets!

Just like before, the temperature inside the alien ship began rising.

AlaHanDrea opened a viewing screen for all to see and hear.

Screams from the alien ship could be heard all over, as they began to cook inside of the ship!

Leon headed back for the ground as quickly as he could. Once landed, he ran to William and Bjorn with AlaHanDrea hot on his tail! They all 4 put their hands together and shot a super beam at the ship, blowing it into space dust, just like the one before it!

Cheers rose up all across the land!

The soldiers were in awe of the toddler!

An entire army of beasts followed a toddler into battle!

A little baby girl!

A little, baby girl that saved the lives of the pilots!

They had a newfound respect for the baby queen.

After that day, soldiers began to come over to the side of the beasts, in groves, as the truth spread like juicy gossip at a PTO meeting.

———————

Chapter 14

AlaHanDrea's 3rd birthday was celebrated to the fullest! Time passed very quickly for the new mixed communities and before they knew it, the baby queen was celebrating her 6th birthday!

Quakes, as well as weather events, were beginning to happen at alarming rates!

One morning shortly after her birthday celebration, AlaHanDrea woke up in a near panic!

"Mister Jax! Mister Jax!" She called out but got no response.

"Prince Harmon!" She cried out, stomping her little foot. "Yes? You summoned me? Well, hello there, little girl. You sure are a pretty little thing. Was it you that summoned me?" Mr. Jax asked her.

"Yes, was me. We all gonna die & is all your fault! Is your job to not let this happen!

You need to move me, my creatures and people, and you need to do it right now!" AlaHanDrea told him.

"What are you talking about sweetie? How are we all gonna die?" He asked her, not knowing quite what to think.

"You mean, you still don't know? Geeesh! Our galaxy is colliding with another galaxy! How do you not know this?" She drew a rectangle in the air and a viewing screen appeared. She ran time lapse video and showed him just what she was talking about!

Panic coursed through his entire being as it sunk in as to what he was seeing!

"See? You need to move us First!

We die and you all die!

Starting with you and your family!

We move today!" She demanded.

Jax tried to pop out to go see his brother, but was unable to move! He was a watcher, yet this little girl was powerful enough to hold him right where he stood!

"You go when I say you can go", she said on a low tone that said she meant business.

"Of course, my apologies. What's your name, little one?" He asked her.

"I, am Queen AlaHanDrea!

So named by the angels of God himself!

Here is a list of all of my creatures and people's. Don't leave any out. If we are not transported first, I will destroy the tunnels... while they are full! Do I make myself perfectly clear?" The ground shook to emphasize the fact that she meant business!

"You do, I hear you. But please know, I must alert my brethren. Billions of lives are on the line! Please understand," he pleaded.

"I understand. Hurry." She instructed.

"I will, I promise to be right back and begin moving y'all."

"I know you will be right back, because I will bring you back myself!" She said, very matter of factly.

Then, released her hold on him.

Prince Harmon put out an urgent, return to planet, call.

All scouts were to return immediately!

The great hall of the ancient planet was filling up quickly.

Prince Harmon sat at the head of the long table, next to his brother, Raynar's, throne. Raynar had held the throne for only a short time, during a trial period, set forth by his father...preparing him to take over primary rule.

Raynar sent for his father and grandfather's to return at once!

When Raynar stepped out of his quarters to take his place at the head of the long table, it occurred to him, that would be the last time he would be addressing his population in the sacred hall.

A tear escaped, rolling down his cheek, as he walked over to his throne.

Raynar stood, looking out over the congregation, staff in hand...

"Brethren, it is with great sorrow that we address you today. My brother has been made aware of some disturbing news. I'll let him tell you. Jax, it's all yours," Raynar passed his brother the staff.

"Brethren, it is with a heavy heart that I tell you, our galaxy is about to be no more.

The currents that steer our galaxies shifted, un-noticed by any of us, putting us on a direct collision course with the M19 Galaxy.

We have precious little time to try to save as many lives as we can. This will be the only meeting that we have before the evacuation begins.

I must make you aware of the urgency.

Normal protocol will not be followed, in that we cannot afford to take a complete species before starting on another ... we must take all that we can take, as quickly as we can take them, and move them, as quickly as we can move them.

2 teams per planet, please. We have very little time!

God's speed, brethren!

Jax sat back down, a sign the meeting was adjourned.

Raynar was walking back to his chamber. He turned and asked Jax, "Well? You coming?"

Jax looked out over at the great hall, watching as his brethren hurried off to begin the evacuation of 2 complete galaxies.

"Ya, I'm coming, bother," he said as he rose to his feet.

Jax closed the door to his brothers chamber, so they wouldn't be disturbed.

"Jax, how did we manage to miss this? We're watchers!" Raynar asked his little brother.

"We just got too comfortable... we forgot how fragile all life is. We got too used to being safe and at the top of the food chain. We forgot that we, too, are fragile," his brother told him.

Ground fog announced the arrival of the True king and the grandfather's.

The life span of watcher was great... Very close to eternal...

There were many grandfather's...

"Father! Is good to see you!" Raynar said to his father.

"Skip the formalities, my son's, tell me about this super baby and the situation we are in."

They filled their father and grandfather's in on what they knew to be true. All of them felt guilty for not having noticed sooner. They scolded themselves for not looking deeper to see what was responsible for all of the quakes and weather.

The king said, "Jax, I want you personally to take that baby girl to Taurus 9. Let the dragons deal with her. I don't like being threatened! In case she survives, you stay behind and keep an eye on her! She needs monitored! Especially, if she survives the dragons!

We'd kill her now, if we didn't owe the child our lives!

I'd kill her anyway, but, the counsel of father's say no. I will not go against our grandfather's.

If she does survive the dragons, that only proves that we placed her correctly.

Scouts will move her list, as she has requested, so says the counsel, not me. I'd kill them all just for being her friends.

Jax, take her as soon as you...." He was interrupted when Jax vanished.

Raynar said, "looks like the baby was ready for him to go back."

"I don't like that child! And I don't Trust that child! She is trouble walking! I say we kill her and be done with her!" The king said.

His father spoke up, "if you do, you will die as a result.

You Know the Law!

She now owns us all!

She plucked us from the Jaws of certain death, we belong to her now!

You know the law, son, you know the law!

Hopefully, she does not know the law and take advantage of us... All we can do now is to pray... And MOVE!

I vote for the Milky Way, all in favor..."

"Well, hello again, little one. Are you ready to go? Scouts are already arriving to evacuate your list, according to your rules. I am personally escorting you in your very own tunnel. We are going to a place called Taurus 9. You will love it there! It's perfect for a creature as powerful as you."

"You were taking too long."

"Yes, I'm sorry for that. My father And grandfather's arrived and had questions for me.

Actually, I owe you a thanks for getting me out of there. I would have had to wait until my father excused me and he can be a bit long winded."

"You're welcome, now, if you're certain my creatures and people are being evacuated, let's go. Now.

Right now!"

He took her little hand and walked her into the transport tunnel.

"AlaHanDrea, time has no meaning in here. Time is only relevant to a planet spinning around it's star. That does not exist here. The further away from the moon we get, the faster time on that moon seems to pass. In other words, you will get to witness the vast explosions once the stars begin to explode," Jax explained.

"These tunnels are cool! I didn't know they are so clear! I can see everything! Wow! Is that our galaxies?" She asked.

"Yes, look at them merging!"

"My creatures!" She cried.

"Oh, no, sweet girl, years have already passed on Ion 6. All of your creatures have long sense been gone from there. See, time has no meaning here, just relax, we will be there soon enough,"Jax explained.

"Are those tunnels to?" She asked, looking at the transparent noodle looking things in space.

"Yes, those are your creatures going to the same place you're going," he explained.

"I'm tired, very sleepy, will you please hold me?" She asked, looking up at him.

"Who could refuse such a request, sure, I'll hold you, sweet girl, come here," he said as he placed her on his hip.

She drifted in and out of sleep, mesmerized by the wonders of space, asking too many questions to answer. The most asked question being, "are we there yet?"

Feeling them slow way down, made her wake up.

"Where are we, are we there yet?" She asked, then yawned.

"Yes we are, we're orbiting looking for a place to land and I think I just found it," Jax answered her.

"Oooh, Mr. Jax, Mr, Jax! What are those magnificent creatures? Oooh! Oooh! I want one! I want one!" She exclaimed.

"Sweet girl, those are dragons. Dragons rule this world. They're flying up here checking us out. They want to see who's arriving on their planet. That's okay, I made us invisible so they can't see us. We will be on the surface in a moment," he explained.

AlaHanDrea was in awe of all of the thick, plush greenery, flowing fresh water and abundance of wilderness. She'd never seen a place so alive! So wild and free...

"This place is so beautiful! Wow! I get to live here? And with all of my creatures? Yippy! I love it!" She squealed.

"Yes, this is your new home!" Jax answered.

Ground fog announced the arrival of Raynar.

"Raynar! Great to see you! I'm a bit surprised, but glad, none the less. What brings you here?" Jax asked his brother.

Raynar didn't say a word, he just walked over to his brother, touched AlaHanDrea on her forehead, putting her in a deep sleep, then asked his brother, "Jax, do you not wonder why you're still holding the child? Now, don't freak out and don't panic, I need for you to remain calm. Healix!" Raynar called out, summoning their big brother and healer to the watchers, as well as to the dragons.

Jax was confused, to say the least .

"Hello bro, what seems to be the... Whoa! Oh Dayum! Jax, dude, you seem to have a baby humanoid girl sticking out of your chest!" Healix exclaimed.

"Thanks bro, I hadn't told him yet," Raynar told Healix.

""What?" Jax asked in a panic.

"Stay calm, let me see what I can do. Oh boy... Looks like the child is absorbing you. Be glad she's not faster. Raynar, you knocked her out?" Healix asked.

"Ya, I thought it best. Hoped it would slow her down a bit. Now what are we going to do?"

Jax was afraid to move. He stood frozen in terror at the thought of dying. Watchers rarely died.

"Brother, please help me. I don't want to be absorbed!" Jax pleaded.

"I'm sorry bro, I'm not sure I know how to do this without killing you both!"

"Hey! Hi there, Raynar, long time, no... Whoa! Why does Jax have a humanoid girl child sticking out of his chest? More to the point, why is Queen AlaHanDrea sticking out of his chest?"

King Neptune asked his old friends.

"Here, move out of the way, let me do this," King Neptune instructed.

"What are you going to do about it?" Healix asked.

"You seem to forget that I'm a God. Now, are you going to stand there talking, or are you going to get out of my way and let me do what needs done?" King Neptune asked them.

They stepped back and let him do his thing.

"Damn, Jax, ol boy, ya really got yourself in a pickle here, let me see what I can do, now, hold really still, you wouldn't want me pulling the wrong things out, now, would you?" Neptune slipped his hands inside Jax chest as tho there was an opening in his chest.

He began pulling and tugging. "This may take me a minute, thanks for choosing to move my people and I, we really appreciate it," Neptune remarked.

"Don't thanks us," Raynar said, "the thanks goes to that baby girl you're pulling out of my little brother.

See, you didn't qualify this time.

You made zero effort to get along with the dry landers. God even gave you the ability to come out of the sea and wear legs, yet, you still made zero effort to learn to get along! How many fleets of ships did you sink? Huh? Learning to get along was not a mere suggestion! If not for that baby girl, you'd be extinct right now. She named you specifically, then your population... you owe her your life, ol boy. You belong to her, now. She plucked you from the Jaws of certain death. She owns you." Raynar told him.

"I suppose I should be more careful, then."

He began speaking in low tones where no one else could hear him, then, he suddenly went stumbling backwards as she released Jax and they were separated. Healix and Raynar rushed to their brother side to catch him as he collapsed to the ground, unconscious.

Healix began attempts to resuscitate his little brother. It wasn't looking very good for Jax. AlaHanDrea walked over and touched Jax forehead. He began to cough, then struggled to sit up.

AlaHanDrea just stood there, staring at the ground. Looking all guilty.

Raynar went over to her, "hello there, I'm Mr Jax big brother, Raynar. Thank you for saving all of us. I just can't thank you enough for saving the billions of lives that you saved by alerting us to the danger we were facing!

We are not angry or upset with you in any way. I appreciate you turning loose of my little brother. I'm quite fond of him and would have missed him terribly. None of us blame you for wanting to possess his power."

"I have more power than he does," she replied, then looked up and locked eyes with Raynar, allowing him to look deep inside of her... he had to force himself to break free. "Wow! You sure do! Well, you're just a little power house, now, aren't you , baby girl! I sure hope that you and I can be friends.

My father wants me to stay here in case you might need me for something.

Jax and I both have been appointed as guardians. So, I really do hope that we can be friends.

Who knows, when you grow up, maybe we can even be better than just friends...only time will tell..."

AlaHanDrea continued to look at the ground. Raynar got the impression that she was feeling kind of angry. She didn't seem very happy about having Mr Jax pulled away from her.

Neptune went to her jend knelt down, " Baby girl, I sure do love you!"

She looked up with a little smile and hugged his neck, then whispered in his ear, "I love you, too, but, if you ever interfere when I'm absorbing someone again, I will kill you where you stand, got it?"

He pulled away, looked her in the eyes and said, "yes, I got it. It won't happen again, your majesty," then he turned to Jax, "I'm not the only one that got a second shot at life today, if it happens again, call someone else, I'm out of the business!

Just remember ol man, you owe me one!" With that, he jumped in the nearby pool of a water fall, shifted, then splashed the water with his tail fin as he swam away...

"We aren't mad at you, sweet girl.

Are you going to be o.k?

Sweetie, it might be to your advantage to shrink yourself to very tiny for awhile. It will keep you safe, tho, we have no doubt that you can take care of yourself, but just the same, it may be best for you to remain tiny for awhile.

We need to get ourselves settled in, if, you no longer need us..." Raynar said to her.

"I'm fine," was all that she said.

Chapter 15

"Braynar, bro, you've been staring at that visions pond for hours, what gives?" Keithen asked his big brother.

There's something up there, spinning webs all up in my berry bush. It flies.

Flying things don't spin webs.

It flies and its spinning webs... in my berry bush.

Go up and shoo it away, squish it or something, would you, little bro?" Braynar asked.

"Ya, sure, I was going that way anyway. Suppose I should change first, look less scary.

I think that was ol Mr. Jax we saw coming in earlier. He probably dropped off some weird alien creatures."

"Well, just be careful, then, little bro. Don't want the parents all yelling at me and shit..." Braynar told him.

"Ya, thanks for the concern, be right back..."

Keithen shifted to man state and went up to have a look.

He decided to use a different entrance than the cave behind the water fall, at least until he found out what it was.

AlaHanDrea froze, she heard someone or something coming up the path.

The tiny queen fluttered over to a Boulder, next to the water fall, where she could get a better view.

What she saw, was a very handsome young man, very muscular & tall and he was headed her way.

He seemed to be looking in the bushes, inspecting her web work.

"O.K. little web maker, I know you're around here somewhere, I'm not going to hurt you, I came up to say hello.

Where are you, little web maker?"

"I'm right here, look up," she said, taking him by surprise.

"Oh, there you are. Well, aren't you the prettiest little thing... Where did you come from?" Keithen asked her.

"I'm from Ion 6.

I just got here.

Ion 6 is dead.

It blew up."

"Our galaxy collided with another galaxy.

Mr. Jax brought me here," she explained.

"Ah, just as I suspected. Ya, I know Mr. Jax, we've met before.

He's friends with my parents.

My name is Prince Keithen, what's yours?"

"I, am Queen AlaHanDrea." She replied.

"Queen... Impressive. Very impressive!

Well, Queen AlaHanDrea, welcome to Taurus 9."

"Thank you, Keifen."

He smiled at the way she pronounced his name.

She smiled back, then asked him if he'd like a glass of nectar wine. He agreed.

She produced 2 goblets, poured them full, then grew his goblet to his size.

"I love your magic, AlaHanDrea.

Oooh, and this nectar is heavenly!

Wow!

This is really good.

You made this?" He asked.

"Uh huh, yep, I sure did," she answered, rather smugly.

"Well, this is very good! I would like it very much if my big brother could try some, too."

She made a barrel appear, then grew it to his size. He thanked her and reduced it back to small and put it in his pocket. She smiled at his use of magic.

"You see that cave under the falls? That's the entrance to a dragons home," Keithen told her.

She squealed with excitement. "Really? Oh boy, oh boy! I saw a dragon when we first got here! They are magnificent! I love them so much! I want one of my very own!

How cool!

A dragon lives in there!" She was so excited, she could barely contain herself.

"Well, sweet girl, dragons aren't pets, dragons rule this world," Keithen explained.

"Oh, I won't stop it from ruling anything, I just want one of my very own! I will love it so much! And it will love me back, too!"

"O.k. well, we'll see about that... You never know... Stranger things have been known to happen. This is the Dragon's front yard and that's his berry bush right there ," he began explaining, but was interrupted by her excitement.

"Well, Mr. Dragon shouldn't mind my living here.

For one, I'm very tiny and I'm much safer living in a dragons yard.

I'm an orphan, ya know, and all alone, except for some creature friends that should be arriving very soon.

I sing really pretty and I make nectar wine, so, what's not to love about me? I'm also very powerful and can protect Mr. Dragon, keep him from harm... Ya, once he gets to know me, he will love me, too!" She explained.

Keithen just gave a little laugh, "o.k. tiny one, I hear you.

So, You, are going to protect a mighty dragon and keep him from harm?"

"Oh yes, I sure will!" She said, in earnest.

"Well, it's very nice to meet you, Queen AlaHanDrea.

Such a pretty name for such a beautiful, tiny girl. May I ask, how old are you? "

"I'm 6 years old!"

"Well, you're a big girl, now, aren't you!

I have to get going, but, I live very close by and will see you often, neighbor," he said.

Just as he turned to leave, she fluttered over, landed on his shoulder and kissed him on his cheek, then fluttered back over to the boulder, blushing.

"Oh, well... Thank you! Thank you very much! That was really nice...

I'll see you real soon, my new tiny friend."

She watched him turn and walk away, feeling really good about making her first friend in her new home.

She had her first real crush...

"Well? What is it? You sure spent enough time visiting with it!" Braynar said.

"First off, it's a she. A 6 inch high, 6 year old, gorgeous, humanoid orphan.

She's from Ion 6. Apparently, their Galaxy collided with another galaxy." Keithen told his brother.

"Oh wow! 2 galaxies collided?

There must have been mass evacuations!

That means, if Mr Jax brought her here, there will be a whole lot more refugees landing soon. We'd better alert the flock, call mom and dad and the royal guard," Braynar said.

"Sure, I agree, but that can wait a minute, taste this nectar she makes, careful tho, she called it wine," Keithen told Braynar.

"Oh, that's good!

I mean, that's really good! Ya, we can send them a message.

I don't see what harm it could do to let her stay in our yard, after all, you said she's only 6 years old, just a baby, and an orphan, to boot...

What kind of souls would we be if we chased that pretty little girl off," Braynar said.

"Her name is Queen AlaHanDrea."

"Queen?"

"That's what she said!"

"I'm going up to meet this queen for myself!"

"As you should, especially since she plans to protect you from harm!" Keithen teased.

"Oh ya? Well, that's awful nice of her," he chuckled, then shifted to man state.

"I take it you didn't tell her that we are dragons," Braynar asked Keithen.

"Na, I thought I'd wait to tell her that part. She wants to catch a dragon and keep him as her very own," Keithen giggled...

"Well Bro, if you're a good boy, maybe she'll scratch your belly and make your leg wiggle," they both cracked up laughing as they headed up to the surface.

They opted to use the entrance by the bush Keithen used the first time he went up to meet the little intruder.

AlaHanDrea froze when she heard a rustling in the bushes, then quickly fluttered up to the boulder again.

She saw her new friend and a very handsome, much bigger fella was with him.

"Now, where is my tiny new friend?

AlaHanDrea!

Where are you?

Oh! There you are, up on your Boulder.

Queen AlaHanDrea, this is my brother, Prince Braynar," Keithen said, as he introduced them.

"I'm pleased to meet you, your majesty," Braynar said to her, with a little bow of respect.

"Pleased to meet you, as well, your highness," she said with a curtsy, blushing.

"You're right, Keithen, she is very beautiful!

It will be a pleasure watching her grow up! Welcome to Drakonia,, AlaHanDrea.

We are glad to have you here with us.

Please, feel free to make your home here, for as long as you wish.

If you require a house, please, just let us know and we will arrange for one to be built for you.

My brother tells me you're an orphan, please accept my condolences. I'm sorry for your loss. Please consider this your home now," Braynar smiled at her and she blushed a deep red.

"You're very kind, both of you are. Thank you for the warm welcome!

I do require a house. I prefer my house up in the trees.

These are much bigger than the trees of Ion 6, but then, Ion 6 was the moon that orbited Zinith 6, the home of the watchers," she explained.

"Wait, what?

Zinith 6 was destroyed? Seriously?" Raynar asked, startled by what he was hearing.

"Yes, it was.

The entire galaxy was ripped to shreds.

Too many stars to count, exploded. Others, were slung out into space. We could see it all happening from the transport tunnels.

It was unbelievable and strangely beautiful to watch.

So much destruction!

I can only hope that most creatures made it out.

I'm sure there were way too many left behind.

It's the watchers fault, you know.

They really dropped the ball on that one!

They didn't even know about it until I told them to move me and my creatures and people, or, I'd destroy them all!

Even then, I had to show it to them on a viewing screen.

They had very little time to evacuate 2 full galaxies...

So much life lost, all because they failed to see what was right there for them to see ..."

"Oh wow.

That is so sad!

They must be very grateful to you for alerting them!"

"I guess they are.

I dunno, you can ask them, if ya want.

They are still here.

Mr Jax, his brother, Raynar and his brother, Healix are still here.

They live here now.

Their father made them my guardians."

"Oh really?" Braynar said, then, " Keithen .."

Braynar was interrupted by his little brother, "Already called them, bro, already called them..."

AlaHanDrea got so excited when she looked up and saw dragons flying over head...

A moment later, King George and Queen Isabel were walking up the path. Braynar introduced them to the baby queen and filled them in on everything she had just told them.

"Raynar is here? Living on Taurus 9?" Isabel asked.

"Yes ma'am, he is. It was supposed to be just Mr. Jax, but, I was a bit of a naughty girl and was absorbing Mr. Jax and Raynar came, then Healix came, but they couldn't make me let go, so, King Neptune, from Ion 6, came up and pulled me out of Mr. Jax and I didn't say I was sorry... Probably because I was only sorry I didn't get to finish.

I was too slow, but, next time, I won't be so slow.

So, their daddy made all 3 sons stay here with me. We got here this morning."

They all had shocked looks on their faces. They didn't quite know what to say to this 6 inch high girl child that claimed to be more powerful than watchers!

Ground fog announced the arrival of either an angel or a watcher. They knew it wasn't God, there was no blinding light.

"Hello George ... Isabel... You're looking good..." Raynar said.

"Raynar..." Isabel said, breathlessly.

George spoke up, "Isabel, why don't you and Raynar go for a walk, I'm sure you have a ton to talk about."

"Yes, George And thank you. I love you, George."

"I love you, too, Isabel."

Then, George saw Healix, "Healix! Good to see you, ol boy! It's been a minute! How are you?"

"Hello George, great to see you again."

"If you kids will excuse us, it was great meeting you, AlaHanDrea!" George said, as he walked off with Healix.

Later that evening, long after the baby queen had spun a cocoon to sleep safely in, George returned to see his son's.

"Well boys, what she says is true.

From what Healix tells me, that tiny little girl is a huge powerhouse!

She was absorbing Jax & he didn't even know it! According to Helix, billions of creatures all owe that child their lives.

She knew those galaxies were colliding, before anybody else did! And... she made sure that those loyal to her, were moved first.

She's quite an amazing creature.

Her parents were created in a laboratory, by scientists doing genetic coding, DNA testing, gene splicing, that sort of thing.

She's a combination of many, many species, which, accounts for her great power.

Don't let her physical size fool you.

From what I'm to understand, she is beyond amazing...

I've been told that the child has no fear in her.

She has a nation of her own, made up of a variety of species, to include some humans.

Most of her citizens, fear her as much as they love her.

They call that little girl Queen, because she is a Queen!

She's flown into battle against alien invasions at only 2 years old and come out victorious!

As an infant, she battled an entire cluster of giant spider, by herself, slaughtering them all with very little effort.

And, she has a blood lust!

I'm also told she's an extremely dangerous creature.

She has fangs, as well as extremely deadly venom.

A creature was bitten and didn't last 30 seconds before they convulsed and died.

She is to be handled with extreme caution and care.

Healix told me that she can inhale a full-grown human male faster than you can say boo!

She turns them to vapor and inhales them!

So just be careful and please...

don't piss her off ...

Ever..."

Chapter 16

Isabel led Raynar to her favorite cave, using her magic to create a quick, comfy lair for them to be alone in... He had been gone for far too long!

(Life had become very complicated, of course, life has a way of doing that from time to time!)

"Raynar, I can't believe that your finally here!

I have missed you, so, so much!" Isabel said, as soon as they were alone.

Raynar stopped, turned around, gazed deeply into her eyes, then kissed her the sweetest, most loving kiss... They held onto each other for a while before kissing again. She buried her face on his chest and began to softly cry.

Raynar held her in his arms and just let her cry, with tears rolling down his own cheeks.

They both fell asleep for a while. Crying seems to have that effect on most everyone.

Raynar woke up to Isabel stroking his hair and gently kissing his face. He rolled her over and kissed her very lovingly. Then, he leaned up and said, "we did nothing wrong, Isabel.

It had been many, many years since George was declared dead.

We did nothing wrong...

It's not everyday a dead husband comes walking through the door, hollering, "honey, I'm home". Usually, the dead stay that way.

All of those years, Isabel, we sinned not. Not in that aspect, anyway. Our fathers probably are of a different opinion...

Sweetheart, Everyone believed George to have been killed in that rock slide!

I mean, where was he for all of those years? Why did he not try to reach you and let you know he was still alive? Surely he had to know how worried you'd be after a quake of that magnitude!

How does he justify you not hearing a word from or about him?

Everyone saw him be buried alive!

Why did he not contact you before all of those years had passed?

Why did he wait so many years to suddenly show up, carrying Keithen's lost egg?" Raynar asked...then said, "Baby, I'm so sorry that my father sent me away on that assignment.

It's really all my own fault.

I assumed he'd disapprove of us getting married, since, we are of different species, as well as heirs to thrones... so I never gave him the chance to object...

Or, give us his blessing."

"I cheated him.

I cheated us all.

I guess I thought that once he found out, he'd be forced to accept it...

Boy, did I ever think wrongly...

I was wrong, so wrong to marry behind his back. Please forgive me, my love.

Angering my father was a really bad idea.

I really don't know what I was thinking!

I wanted what I wanted Jend didn't want to be told no...

I'm so sorry that my actions hurt you so! Hurt Us, all of us, so much!"

"Wait, You didn't tell your father we were getting married?

Raynar! How could you not tell him?

I told mine!

I listened to the lectures... Then did what I wanted to do, anyway.

I thought you told your dad!

Well, no wonder he sent you away!

Raynar, I think you should know that you left something with me.

Something extremely valuable..."

"I did?" he asked, feeling confused.

"You did.

An egg.

A spotted egg.

The spotted egg of a male child.

Raynar,

Braynar is Your son."

"What?" He said, stunned...

"Braynar is your son, Boy Raynar, Braynar... He is your boy.

You didn't just leave me, you left me with your child," she explained, feeling the hurt all over again.

"I'm a dad?

Wait, I'm a father?

I made a baby?

We, made a baby?

Braynar?

Really!

My Son?!!?"

"I'm a father!!!" He exclaimed, then grabbed Isabel up and spun her around, then kissed her again.

"Oh, baby, I'm so sorry that I abandoned y'all!

I never meant to!

How can you ever forgive me... ?

I wish I'd have known that we are parents, I'd have been back sooner!

Dad told me that George had come home, so, I hadn't really planned on returning.

Does Braynar know?" Raynar asked her...

"No, he doesn't know, yet.

You weren't planning on returning?

You were just going to stay gone and not even come see me?

We're married, Raynar!

How long have you been back from assignment?

You know what, don't tell me.

No, Braynar does not know.

He accepted George as his father... when George came back, that is.

I fainted when George came through that door, carrying Keithen's egg!

He already knew about Braynar by the time he got home to me.

He understood, said there was nothing to forgive me for.

I simply have 2 husband's now.

It wasn't on purpose, no one planned this, it just is.

And...

You are home now, Raynar.

And ..

You are still My husband!

King Raynar!

You'll stay right here, with me... where you belong!

I am your wife!

You've been gone for way too long as it is!

So, you'll stay right here... with me...

And ...

with George ...

one family.

I have a son with both of you.

I love both of you.

Even if I am very upset with you right now!!!

How would I ever choose?

I'm just as upset with you as I am upset with him! And visa versa!

Both of you deserve a huge kick in the....."

"You and I unite the Dragons and the Watchers, Raynar.

You and George will both reign in your respective kingdoms.

I am Queen, no matter where my throne sits.

And...

After giving it a lot of thought; I thought it best to let you be the one to explain things to your son, Our son, as well as to Keithen," Isabel explained.

"Raynar, you are my husband!

You said you love me! You married me and you just weren't going to come back?

Seriously?" Isabel was a tad bit on the side of upset, to say the least!

"Isabel, my dad told me that George was Back!

He also forbade me to return.

To defy him would have meant my death!

Anyway, I'm back now and I Do love you!

I've always loved you, Isabel!

And... Truthfully,

Your solution is actually the best solution, for us all, to include as an example for the kingdoms, when you stop and think about it.

I just have to learn to share," Raynar teased.

Then said, "Sweetheart, we lead by example.

This is the only fair solution.

And, you're right, it brings our two nations together and bonds them.

Isabel, I love you and I even love that stubborn, incredibly strong, hard headed other husband of yours... my brosband? Broband? Brother hubby?

Guess I should go have a talk with my son, Our son...

Our Son!!!" Raynar said, as he got up to leave to go see Braynar.

The unsuspecting Braynar, was back at his cave, with several members of the royal guard.

Danalli, Franklon, Paulio, Thomlin, Sanders & Craigen, as well as his little brother, Keithen, were all sitting in the lower level of Braynar's cave, discussing strategies for hunting, both for food and for women...

Especially, for women.

Raynar stood and listened for a moment, before letting himself be seen.

"Hey, Bray, dude, can I see you for a moment?" Raynar asked.

Suddenly, loud, shrieking, hysterical, screams rang out!

It was the Tiny, little girl!

She was absolutely hysterical!

The guys all headed for the surface!

Keithen reached her first, "what's wrong, tiny one, what's the matter?" Keithen asked her as she fluttered wildly about, screaming... "They are killing him!

They are killing him!

They are eating him alive!

Aliens!

Aliens are eating him!

Oh No!

Dragons can't see them!" She screamed!

Then, "Well, I can!

I can see them!

Alert the dragons!

Alert the dragons!

Tell them to wait for my signal!

They will know it when they see it!

Tell them to wait for my signal!" She cried out as she flew away screaming, they are a killing a dragon!"

Keithen alerted the flock!

He was first to shift and take position, to wait ...

It wasn't a very long wait!

Moments later, purple dust began falling from the skies!

All of a sudden, the dragons could see swarms of tiny fly looking creatures picking a dragons bones clean!

It infuriated the entire flock!!!

Thousands and thousands of dragons, took to the air to fight against the carnivorous intruders!

Keithen and Danalli spotted AlaHanDrea at the same time!

She was surrounded by a swarm of those things, slamming into her forcefield trying to get to that precious little girl that was making them visible.

They both prayed her shields would hold, took a big, deep breath and blew flames, incinerating the whole swarm that was trying to make a meal of her!

She began to fall from the sky, exhausted from holding up her shields against the flames! Danalli, Keithen and Braynar all flew as quickly as they could, to try to catch the tiny girl!

She landed on Keithen, bounced off and hit Braynar, bounced off and landed smoothly on Danalli, then rolled up in his mane.

Danalli stopped in mid air, reared up, then swelled to super giant size!

He could also see the aliens without the purple powder!

There was a mother ship orbiting in the outer atmosphere!

Danalli headed straight for that mother ship, blanketing the sky with flames as he rushed up to destroy that ship!

Power surged through Danalli like nothing he had ever felt!

The alien ship began sending hundreds of fighter ships to battle the giant dragon, Danalli, to no avail!

The mighty warrior dragon incinerated them all!

Then, he set his focus on the main mother ship!

Without the addition of AlaHanDrea, Danalli was a fierce and mighty warrior, but with her, he was absolutely vicious, taking out that mother ship as if it were a mere toy!

He incinerated it, then turned and swatted the thing with his enormous tail, smashing it into so much dust!

First, Danalli felt AlaHanDrea lose consciousness, then he felt himself roll onto his back, falling towards the planets surface, shrinking back to normal size as he fell.

Braynar, Thomlin, Paulio, Craigen, Franklon and many others , flew as quickly as they could, materialized a giant net, held by all and proceeded to catch their falling hero!

He bounced up off of the net 5 times before they had a secure hold on him. About ten feet later, they were on the ground!

They laid Danalli's net down on the beach. He didn't look good at all. Neither did AlaHanDrea.

The sound of drums parading towards the beach, grabbed everyone's attention...

Thum thump. Thum thump. Thum thump...

The drums sounded like the beating of a heart.

Hundreds of tiny elfen fairies paraded down to the beach, making a circle around the dragon and his tiny passenger.

The fairies were using their magic to keep the dragon and the baby queen alive, beating their hearts for them.

Hours turned to days that turned to weeks. 24/7, the drums beat...

Thum thump. Thum thump.

Creatures from all over, joined in the circle, stomping their feet in the rhythm of a beating heart, if they didn't have a drum, lending themselves to the powerful magic at work.

George and Isabel were beside themselves. They never once left Danalli's side while he lay there, fighting to stay alive.

More than a month later,

Isabel saw it first. Danalli's finger began tapping the beat of the drums!

Then 2 fingers...

He began to shake his head, trying to get up!

Braynar And Paulio helped him get up and shift to man state.

AlaHanDrea rolled out of his hair. Braynar caught her in the palm of his hand.... she was looking very dead.

King Neptune came up out of the sea. He went over and took the tiny child out of Braynar's hand, gently blowing air up her nostrils.

On about the 4th try, AlaHanDrea began to cough and come around.

She was alive!

The rhythm of the tiny drums shifted from the beating of a heart to celebrations!

Cheers rose up from the crowd that had been patiently waiting for the 2 hero's to regain their lives!

Danalli took AlaHanDrea into the palm of his hand and held her over his head in a victory stance!

She threw up her little fist and the cheers got way louder!

A 6 inch high, 6 year old little girl, had just led an army of dragons into battle!

And Won!

The baby girl didn't know when she'd been happier to see her fairies!

It was so good to see them again! They saved her!

She worried that the move would have killed them.

She was so relieved they made it safe and sound to Taurus 9!

Since they made it o.k, she was excited to see her other creatures and humans, too!

They should all be there by now!

She really missed Dane and Athena!

Leon, especially!

He made her feel safe, as well as needed.

Leon was her big, cuddly flying giant lion, & she loved him dearly!

Celebrations had begun for the victory in battle!

They couldn't begin until the hero's were o.k. Now that they were back from the land of the dead, the partying was on... full force!

AlaHanDrea really just wanted to say hello to all of her Ion 6 friends!

The baby Queen took a seat by the royals when she saw her favorite sisters and their husbands!

She Loved watching them dance!

They took dancing very seriously.

Their dancing styles greatly resembled ball room, with lots of acrobatic stunts... Only they did it with wheels on their feet!

Now, dragons were big on romance and were proud of their own dancing abilities, but they had not seen anyone doing it with wheels on their feet before!

Isabel said, "that large group of girls all look a like."

"They are from Ion 6 and are all sisters," AlaHanDrea explained. "They are all triplets. 5 sets of triplets, before their mother went crazy, then died. They are the product of science meddling again. There were more, but the mother killed them. She actually had quads, and octuplets, but killed most of them, because it was much to hard to take care of them all.

All of the boys were killed."

Bears, wolves and lions stepped up, claimed the girls and married them.

"Oh, that's so sad. I don't think I would have liked your Ion 6," Isabel commented.

"No, you probably wouldn't have. All of the sisters married royalty, they did quite well for themselves. They seem to enjoy being married to creatures, too." AlaHanDrea explained.

"Mixed marriages, still not sure how I feel about that. So, are all of the creatures from Ion 6, shifters?"

"Ya, pretty much! Ya know, I first met the sisters when I was 4 years old. They ran away from their step father, who, was trying to sell them to strange men, just not to keep.

So, the girls ran away.

They showed up at my place in the wilderness, told me what happened, so, I killed their step father, as well as some of the men trying to buy them. I ate them all." AlaHanDrea said, rather matter of factly, as tho it were the most natural thing in the world!

Isabel was quiet for a moment, then said, "well, good for you! Nothing wrong with a good meal."

AlaHanDrea smiled at Isabel. "I think I'm really going to like you! When I grow up, we will have so much fun, you and I!"

Her and Isabel both giggled.

Isabel had a feeling the tiny girl was right!

The music began. 15 couples took to the dance floor with their skates on.

They began simple enough, but very quickly got into the more impressive stunt's together. When the song was over, they sat down.

The dragon/men felt as tho they had just been challenged! They grabbed their ladies and took to the dance floor, no skates.

They showed off some pretty impressive dance skills, then sat down at the end of that song.

The sisters and their husbands got back up on the floor and basically copied the dragons, only, on wheels...

When the song ended, they took a seat and smiled at the man dragons...

Before the night was through, dragons were learning to skate! Stating that, "anything they can do, we can do better! We can do anything better than them!"

"No you can't."

"Yes we can!"

Dragons were used to pretty much holding a monopoly on shape shifting on Taurus 9, before the refugees arrived....

That sure all changed in a big hurry...

Lions, as well as all sorts of big cats, bears, wolves, all shape shifters... Crocodiles, mers, flying creatures, all shape shifters...

It was going to take some getting used to for the dragon population...

The dragons developed shifting as a survival skill... the Ion 6 creatures shifted because AlaHanDrea willed it to be so!

The size of the creatures from Ion 6 was also going to take some adjustments. The creatures were giants in comparison to those of Taurus 9!

The royals of Ion 6 were escorted to the table of Dragon Royalty.

Somehow, the conversation kept going back to accounts of the infant Queens victorious battles......

Battles won before she could even walk!

The dragons heard tales of a tiny, brand new infant girl becoming victorious in battles... They heard tales of the infant girl protecting the creatures she loves... Fearless... Strong... Powerful ...and As an infant!

They also heard tales of a newly born girl child, absorbing a Goddess and a scientist! Then, retrieving the soul of her deceased mother for safe keeping.

Had the dragons not personally witnessed the 6 year old little girl flying off into battle, with no thought whatsoever to her own personal safety, they most likely would not have believed the stories they were hearing!

Chapter 17

Raynar finally caught back up with Braynar. He still had not spoken to him since the battle began... the battle, as well as Danalli fighting for his life, had caused their talk to be put on hold.

"Bray, dude, there you are. Hey, I need to talk to you. It's important, dude... Um... Would you mind terribly, uh, following me for a moment? I prefer to talk where we can have absolute privacy," Raynar asked him.

Braynar couldn't imagine what could be so important for Raynar to need to discuss with him.

Curiosity got him and he agreed.

They flew farther than Braynar expected, seriously peaking his curiosity...

They finally landed on a small island, where they could talk with a level of privacy.

"So, Raynar, what's up? Why did you bring me all of the way out here?" Braynar asked him.

"Oh, I don't want to be over heard...

There is just no easy way to say this...

Braynar, remember when George was missing? Well, before you came along, your mother and I got married... "

"Wait, what," Braynar asked.

"Ya, your mother and I got married.

George had been missing for over 35 years... Declared dead for over 35 years!

She had been a widowed Queen for over 35 years!

I love her...so...her and I got married!

I happen to love your mother very much.

We had a baby, Braynar.

I didn't know that at the time.

We had.....

You...

I'm your father..."

Braynar sat in stunned silence, unsure of what to say!

Then, he looked at Raynar, really looked at him, head to foot.

"I see me in you!

I'm a grown ass man, why am I just now hearing about this?" Braynar asked him in a bit of a growl.

"Bray, dude, I just now found out, my own self. Of course, this is the first time I've seen your mother since my father sent me away.

You see, I married Isabel behind his back and it really pissed him off," Raynar admitted.

"So, you lied the lie of omission, your dad found out...

How did you expect to keep a thing like getting married, a secret?

Didn't you realize that he'd be pissed when he found out?

What were you thinking?" Braynar asked.

"That's just it, I wasn't thinking, at least, I wasn't thinking right. I know, I really messed up!"

"Ya think?

Dude, Keithen is like 15 years old!

George has been back for 15 years! I was like 11 when George returned!

Where have you been?

Franklon carried me to hatch in your absence.

He and my mother raised me until George came home!

And no, Franklon was not my mother's lover!

He was her royal guard as a child, he raised her! And he carried me in his pouch, for her.

He helped raise me, for her...

Because you were not here and George was supposed to be dead! Franklon was the one that stood by her... Because both of her husband's left her alone! And yet, you tell me that you loved her?"

"Bray, I don't expect you to understand, heck, I don't really understand it, myself.

My father sent me away and forbade me to return!

He went so far as to set me on the throne early, just to keep me there.

Our planet was destroyed and AlaHanDrea tried to absorb my brother! So, my father sent me back here. Otherwise, had I disobeyed him, he would have destroyed me. Or, at least, that's what he told me.

I heard him instruct the guards to kill me if I attempted to leave.

I was no longer allowed to scout or to relocate, once my initial tour was through. I was basically a prisoner on the throne, as punishment for my sins against him.

I'm not really sure how he's going to feel when he finds out I'm living with my wife back here."

"Wait, what? Mom's leaving George?"

"Oh! No, no Braynar, she isn't leaving George...

No, uh, well, ya see, I'm moving in with both of them..."

"Oh... O.K...?"

"Son, I am so sorry that I lied to my dad, in that I got married without his knowledge. In doing so, I robbed you and your mother, both!

I robbed us all!

My parents, you, Isabel, all of us and I am so, so sorry!

Hopefully, the day will come when you can forgive me...

I can't begin to tell you how all of this makes me feel and how much guilt I'm carrying right now... I can only imagine how it makes you feel! I regret I can't turn the clock back! I mean, I can, but I really can't. It's possible, it's just a really bad idea!

I missed the childhood of my only son! I'm so sorry.

But, so, I'm here now.

Can we try, please?"

"You need to be the one to tell Keithen. Maybe you and George together. Personally, I'd like to be in on that conversation. I have questions for you both and I'm positive my little brother will want to hear the answers as well!

Geeeeez... You're my dad!...

GEEEEEESH! I'm half WATCHER!

Well, No WONDER I'm so much bigger than everyone else!

Don't miss out!

Visit the website below and you can sign up to receive emails whenever Jeri Andrew publishes a new book. There's no charge and no obligation.

https://books2read.com/r/B-A-YGIAB-PBAOC

BOOKS2READ

Connecting independent readers to independent writers.

# About the Author

Having always been accredited with having a vivid imagination, as well as a knack for story telling, it's a dream come true to finally be at a place in life, that allows me the freedom to write and share the stories previously locked away in the recesses of my mind.